Signed
by *Zelda*

ALSO BY KATE FEIFFER

The Problem with the Puddles

Signed by Zelda

KATE FEIFFER

A Paula Wiseman Book

SIMON & SCHUSTER
BOOKS FOR YOUNG READERS

New York London Toronto Sydney New Delhi

SIMON & SCHUSTER BOOKS FOR YOUNG READERS
An imprint of Simon & Schuster Children's Publishing Division
1230 Avenue of the Americas, New York, New York 10020
This book is a work of fiction. Any references to historical events, real people, or real places are used fictitiously. Other names, characters, places, and events are products of the author's imagination, and any resemblance to actual events or places or persons, living or dead, is entirely coincidental.
Copyright © 2012 by Kate Feiffer
SIMON & SCHUSTER BOOKS FOR YOUNG READERS is a trademark of Simon & Schuster, Inc.
For information about special discounts for bulk purchases, please contact Simon & Schuster Special Sales at 1-866-506-1949 or business@simonandschuster.com.
The Simon & Schuster Speakers Bureau can bring authors to your live event. For more information or to book an event, contact the Simon & Schuster Speakers Bureau at 1-866-248-3049 or visit our website at www.simonspeakers.com.
Also available in a Simon & Schuster Books for Young Readers hardcover edition
Book design by Laurent Linn
The text for this book is set in Minister Std.
Manufactured in the United States of America
0413 OFF
2 4 6 8 10 9 7 5 3 1
The Library of Congress has cataloged the hardcover edition as follows:
Feiffer, Kate.
Signed by Zelda / Kate Feiffer—1st ed.
p. cm.
"A Paula Wiseman Book."
Summary: An eleven-year-old aspiring handwriting analyst, a solitary boy, and a talking pigeon solve the mystery of Nicky's missing grandmother.
ISBN 978-1-4424-3331-1 (alk. paper)
ISBN 978-1-4424-3333-5 (eBook)
ISBN 978-1-4424-3332-8 (pbk)
[1. Graphology—Fiction. 2. Grandmothers—Fiction. 3. Missing persons—Fiction. 4. Mystery and detective stories.] I. Title.
PZ7.F33346Si 2012
[Fic]—dc23
2011043905

For Alley, Emma, and Maddy

PART ONE

Grandma Zelda didn't answer her doorbell the first time Nicky rang. The second time, he pressed down on the buzzer and counted to a hundred, although he knew that if Grandma Zelda didn't have her ears in, he could count to a million and she still wouldn't hear him.

Her note had instructed him to sneak out. She'd be expecting him. Nicky turned the door-knob and heard a gulping sound but wasn't sure if it came from him or the door. He pushed. The door swung open, but the doorknob remained behind, in Nicky's hand. "Oh, no," he whispered to himself. "I hope I don't get in trouble for this."

Nicky had a bad habit of getting in trouble. Lately his Time-Out Average (TOA) had spiked to .750, which meant that he did something that earned him a time-out three days out of four. Grandma Zelda was pretty much the only person left that Nicky's dad allowed him to spend time with. "I suppose you can't do anything that will land you in too much hot water with someone so old," his dad had told him.

Grandma Zelda wouldn't care anyway. She didn't believe in time-outs. During their afternoons together she fed Nicky slices of his beyond-favorite Zeldaberry pie and helped him make plans for a sail around the world. "If you meet a pirate, ask about his grandmother," she'd advise. Or she'd tell him a story about the time she once swam under a pirate's ship and scraped a nugget of gold off the keel. "It's around here somewhere, if I could only remember where I put it," she'd say.

Grandma Zelda hadn't left her apartment in over a year, but she used to lead a life of adventure. Nicky couldn't picture his tiny gray-haired grandmother doing any of this, but she once rode a camel across the Sinai desert, and twice she jumped out of an airplane and parachuted into Mongolia. Grandma Zelda's left eye liked to wink when she talked, and she spoke with a Southern drawl, which was unusual for someone who'd grown up in the North. She had so many stories to tell that Nicky figured she kept telling them even when she was alone, even when she was asleep.

• • •

4

Nicky clutched the doorknob and stepped inside Grandma Zelda's apartment. Her walls were covered with photographs and paintings. She kept every picture that Nicky and his sister, Stella, made for her and hung several of them next to paintings by better-known artists. It never felt messy in her apartment but always seemed busy.

Nicky called out for her. "Grandma Zelda?"

"Grandma?" he called out again after he didn't get a response. "Grandma. Grandma Zelda?"

He walked into the kitchen. He waved to the pigeon squatting on the windowsill. He checked for Grandma Zelda in the bedroom. He saw her viola d'amore resting on the bed, alone. Nicky looked around the sides of her bed, in case she had fallen off it. He looked under the bed, in case she'd rolled under it.

He looked for her in the bathroom, the shower, and the cabinets.

"Grandma?"

He pushed his way into her two closets, behind her housecoats and dresses.

"Grandma? Grandma Zelda?"

Back in the hallway.

"Grandma Zelda, is this an April Fools' Day trick?"

"Grandma Zelda?" Nicky called out one final time.

PART TWO

SEVEN MONTHS EARLIER

The Bertels waited on the plane for five hours before takeoff. During the first hour Lucy's parents asked her twelve times, approximately once every five minutes, if she wanted to play a word game with them. Her mother started glancing at her watch mid-way through hour two. Each time she did, Lucy's dad would reach over and gently touch her hand. "That's not going to help, Sarita."

Lucy didn't mind the delay. She was grateful to have more time in Savannah. Every extra minute she got in Savannah meant one less minute of wasting her life in New York.

Lucy's family was leaving Savannah for the following reason, as told to her: "Mom was offered a *great* job at a *great* children's hospital, and Dad had a *great* teaching opportunity at a *great* school that you will be able to attend. Isn't that *great*?" Lucy was being forced to uproot and leave everything she had known for the first and only eleven years of her life. And if that wasn't bad enough, she also lost all respect for the word "great." "Great" was a word she'd once trusted, but when her parents told her they were moving to a *great* new city where she'd have a *great* new life, she realized the word "great" was fundamentally flawed. She started thinking of it as a throwaway word. You know, those words that get used when people don't want to say what they really want to say, so they start using throwaway words.

"Mom was offered a *great* job at a *great* children's hospital, and Dad had a *great* teaching opportunity at a *great* school that you will be able to attend. Isn't that *great*?"

Translated to:

"Mom got a big-deal job as a surgeon at a fancy children's hospital far away from her job at a perfectly fine hospital in Savannah, and Dad managed to find a job teaching math."

"Great," thought Lucy. *Who needs "great"?*

After the pilot apologized for the delay for the seventh time, Lucy asked one of the flight attendants if it would be possible to get a note from him.

"I'm afraid we can't bring notes into the cockpit for security reasons," responded the flight attendant. She hadn't understood Lucy's request.

"Can he write me a note? You know, since we're not flying right now, maybe he has some extra time."

"You'd like the pilot to write a note? What a wonderful way to remember your trip. I will certainly ask him. What's your name, honey?" Lucy thought the flight attendant liked her request. She probably found it more interesting than the other questions she had to answer. "Ma'am, can I have some coffee?" "Miss, when is the plane going to take off?" Those questions.

"My name is Lucy."

"Lucy, I will see what I can do."

A few minutes later the flight attendant returned holding a piece of paper.

"This is for you, Lucy. It's from Captain Hart."

"Thank you." Lucy smiled and reached down into her travel bag. She pulled out a pocket magnifier, a blue fine-point pen, a lime-green notebook with a pink strap that wrapped around it, a date stamp, and a glue stick. She opened the notebook and read, for about the ten trillionth time, the letter her classmates had written on the first page.

Dear Lucy,

Have fun at your new school next year. We hope you fill this handwriting journal with a million handwriting samples. We all want to know if people up north write differently than they do here. Maybe you'll even get your first big case. Don't ever forget your friends from Mrs. Melnick's class. Not that you could. We'll miss you.

Love,

Nina   Jeremy

Katherine   Aidan   Veronica

Nicole   Shelby

Chloe   Thomas

William

They had given her a new handwriting journal as a good-bye, but not forever, present on the last day of school. Lucy had promised herself she wouldn't start filling it up until she moved, so she spent the first few weeks of summer examining the signatures and thinking about how no one should be forced to leave a school that had so much good handwriting, the best of which belonged to the Wrighties, Lucy's three best friends, who, aside from her, were all left-handed. Lefties, otherwise known as left-handed people, had a reputation for messy handwriting, but the Wrighties were not typical lefties, as anyone who saw their writing would confirm. "Now you'll be Wrighties without a righty," said Lucy when she told them she was moving.

On August 1 Lucy decided to hide the journal from herself, hoping she'd forget where she put it and that her parents would agree that they couldn't possibly move without her new handwriting journal. Her mother found the not-quite-lost handwriting journal ten days after Lucy had hidden it, and now Lucy was sitting on a plane that didn't seem to want to leave Savannah either.

Lucy turned to a blank page, stamped the date, and pasted the captain's note onto it. She immediately thought about ripping it out. Maybe if she ripped it out the plane would never take off, and if the plane never took off, they wouldn't be able to move. Only, before she had a chance to do anything, the captain's voice piped in, loud and clear. There was no possible way to misunderstand him; they were taxiing to the runway.

"This is Captain Hart. I'd like to thank you again for your patience. We apologize for the long delay. I am happy to finally be able to report that we have been cleared for takeoff, so please fasten your seat belts."

Lucy tugged on the long strap to her already fastened seat belt. She looked out the window and said good-bye to the only place she had ever lived. She squeezed her eyes shut and felt the plane moving. When she opened her eyes, she whispered, "Don't worry. I'll be back soon."

She pulled the small rectangular magnifying glass out of its case and flicked the light on. She looked at the captain's note through it and chuckled. *Yes*, she thought, *I can definitely see why he's a pilot. Captain Hart's lines slanted upward, as if they were taking off into the air.*

August 30

Dear Lucy,

I hope you have a wonderful flight.

Sincerely yours,

Captain C. Hart

2:20 p.m.
West 68th Street, Building Lobby

Nicky heard the banging and drilling all summer long. It didn't bother him. He actually kind of liked the noise. Apartment 6D, which was one apartment below his, had been empty for a year. He didn't care that someone new was moving in. He just hoped they weren't complainers. The last people who'd lived there had sure liked to complain.

He watched the movers trying to maneuver couches, tables, beds, bureaus, and boxes through the front door and into the service elevator.

"Do you need any help?" he asked.

"Sure do, kid," one of the movers replied. "We could really use another strong guy. This family didn't forget to pack a thing. Unfortunately, though, we can't take you up on your offer. Union rules."

"Oh," said Nicky. "I forgot about that. Do you know who's moving in?"

"Don't know a thing, except their stuff came from Savannah, Georgia."

"Cool," said Nicky. "Maybe they'll have Southern accents. My grandma has a Southern accent."

"I reckon they will," said the mover. "Hey, kid, when does school start?"

"Tomorrow," replied Nicky. "I don't care, though. I had a terrible summer."

"Sorry to hear that. Really sorry to hear that."

"Yeah," said Nicky. "It's a drag when you're stuck in the city and there's no one to do anything with."

"You got brothers or sisters?"

"One sister, sometimes. She acts like I don't exist most of the time, so I call her my sometimes sister."

"I had one of those, kid. I'm thirty-three now, and she still doesn't talk to me," said the mover.

"I spent most of the summer with my grandma and a—" Nicky bit his lower lip. "Never mind. You sure I can't help you?"

"Sorry, kid."

The elevator door opened and the movers pushed a dolly filled with boxes into it. Nicky looked up at the bronze panel above the elevator door, and watched the numbers light up—1, 2, 3, 4, 5, 6.

"Pigeon," he said, now that no one was around to hear him. "I spent the summer talking to a pigeon."

7:04 p.m.
West 68th Street, Building Lobby

"This is where we're living now." Lucy walked over to one of the black-and-white photographs that lined the cream-colored walls of her new building. "I don't think this is a very good picture. So this is where we're living now," she repeated.

"Is that a question or a comment?" asked her father.

"I don't know. Maybe just a statement of doom."

Lucy's mother had fallen asleep during the cab ride from the airport to the city and hadn't quite regained her bearings. At least that was the excuse she used after putting her suitcase down directly in front of her and then taking a step and tripping over it. Lucy looked at her mother sprawled across the floor and said, "You see. Doom. Mom, are you okay?"

"I think I'm fine," said Dr. Bertel. "Just a bit groggy after all the travel. The good news is that it appears we've moved into a building with a clean floor. Honey, can you please come here and give me a hand."

"It's good to get things, like the first tumble, out of the way quickly. Lucy, I want you to be in charge of breaking the first glass. I'll make sure to be the first one to get locked out of our apartment," said Mr. Bertel.

Lucy tried not to smile but couldn't help herself. "Can I overflow the bathtub first?"

"Only if I can have the honor of drinking the first glass of water," said Dr. Bertel, now standing.

"I'll bake the first batch of cookies," said Lucy.

"And I'll burn the first batch," added her mother.

Lucy caught her father's eye. They nodded and said "That's true" in tandem.

"May I be the first to push the button for the elevator?" Lucy asked.

"Absolutely," said Mr. Bertel. "And you can be the first to push the six button."

The Bertels continued stringing together a list of firsts (first to open the door, first to walk inside, first to find the red velvet chaise longue, first to sing a song) while Lucy entered the room that would be called hers. She flicked on the light and walked over to the window. "Mom, Dad," she called out, "I'm the first to see a real-life New York City pigeon on my windowsill."

MONDAY, AUGUST 31
7:05 a.m.
West 68th Street, Apartment 6D

The first day of school should be declared a national holiday and be observed by canceling school for the day. At the very least the first day of school should never come the morning after sleeping in two new beds (first her bed and then her parents' bed after a freaky thumping noise on her ceiling in the middle of the night sent Lucy fleeing into their room) in a new apartment in a new city. When Lucy woke up, she made these points to her parents, to no avail.

"It's not a good day for this first," she said.

"Missing the first day of school would be like skipping your birthday," said her mother.

"No, Mom. Actually, it's kind of the opposite of that."

"Well, it's my first day of school too, and I need to get there early, so if you're coming with me, you better eat breakfast and get yourself dressed quickly." Her dad looked serious. "Lucille," he said. Wow, he was really serious.

"I can't," moaned Lucy. "I didn't get enough sleep. You woke me up too early."

As usual Lucy's dad had woken up before the roosters, or whatever they had here instead of roosters. Muggers, maybe? He claimed that he'd tried to be quiet, but no one really attempting to be quiet sounded like a marching band. Her dad's quiet consisted of clanging pots and pans together, breaking glasses, and making teapots whistle.

"Lucy, I need to get in early today. I should have been here a week ago. Please pull yourself together," said her father.

"I can't. I haven't adjusted to the new time zone yet. I need a day at home to adjust," replied Lucy.

"This isn't a new time zone," Mr. Bertel reminded her.

"I haven't adjusted to the new temperature zone."

"Same temperature," said Lucy's mother. "It's lovely out, just like it was in Savannah yesterday."

"I've never slept on the sixth floor before. I need to adjust to a new height zone. I feel dizzy."

"Honey, it's going to be fine. Think of it this way—you'll have a whole new school filled with handwriting just waiting to be analyzed. Think of all those letters." Dr. Bertel smiled; she knew she was saying the right thing. "Why don't you ask the kids in your class for handwriting samples."

"Handwriting samples." The two words everyone in Lucy's family used whenever they wanted her to do something she didn't want to do. "You need to get a tetanus booster," her mom, who was a doctor and knew better than anyone how much shots hurt, would say. "No, I don't. I just won't step on any rusty nails," Lucy would reply. "You can get a *handwriting sample* from the nurse," her mom would then add, and off Lucy would go for the shot.

Imagine a dog walking away from a tasty bone. There's a far greater chance of that happening than Lucy walking away from the gift of a handwriting sample. During the past five years she had filled twenty-six handwriting analysis journals with signatures—almost two her first year collecting, four during the second year, seven both the third and fourth year, and six so far this year. She had amassed so many handwriting analysis journals with just handwriting samples, and not signatures, that they didn't all fit in her move-to-New-York boxes. (Her parents were somewhat reluctant, but nevertheless, they agreed to let her store them, under lock and key and twenty-four-hour camera surveillance, in Savannah Safeguards Storage. Lucy took this as a good sign they'd be going back to Savannah soon. Maybe the only good sign.)

Handwriting samples. She smiled at the thought of getting signatures from people in the North. *At least I'll find out if it's true that kids in New York write really quickly,* thought Lucy. Lucy believed you could learn a lot about a person by looking at their handwriting, enough to figure out if they were nice or mean, old or young, happy or sad, and honest or dishonest. She and the Wrighties had one guiding principle—*You are what you write*—and she'd find out soon, too soon if you asked her, what kinds of writing and what kinds of kids she'd be stuck with for the next year. *Getting new handwriting samples might be the only good thing to come out of moving,* thought Lucy.

Lucy planned on becoming the world's leading expert on handwriting. She'd be so sought after that someday the FBI, the CIA, and Interpol would contact her for help with their most mind-boggling cases. Already she had solved several tough cases that the Wrighties had staged for her.

I have Mary

U can have her back

only $5,000

Case #10-05-17-064DLB. Kidnapping.

The FBI, or in this case the Wrighties, wearing neckties and black horn-rimmed glasses, delivered a heat-sealed envelope to Lucy. Lucy put on white cotton gloves and carefully removed a ransom note from the envelope. She photocopied the note, then picked the original up using a set of tongs, and lifted it in the air. Holding a flashlight at an acute angle to the paper, she scanned the note from top to bottom and found the words "pump," "wedge," and "high heels" indented into the paper. Someone, possibly the kidnapper, had written them on a piece of paper that was placed over the ransom note. Lucy carried the note into an empty closet and flicked on a black light. The last few words in the note glowed red, while the other words looked blue. Lucy thanked the black light for once again being such a helpful tool and making it easy for her to see that the ransom note was written using two different pens. Lucy put the note in an airtight bag, turned off the black light, and returned to the main lab. Working with the photocopy of the note, she measured the height and width of every letter and the amount of space between the letters. After she meticulously examined the details of the note, she presented her findings.

"See the shoes on the toes of the *i* and *y*s. Notice the spirals on *u* and *r*. I think our kidnapper enjoys shopping for shoes. There's a small coffee stain and the kidnapper used two pens. To the naked eye you can't tell, but under a black light, it's as clear as day. My theory is that the kidnapper broke one of her cat-scratch-long fingernails while writing the ransom note and got so upset that she spilled her coffee. After she cleaned up, she couldn't find the pen she used, so she got another one. I think the kidnapper is hiding Mary at a department store. She planned on shopping for shoes and getting a mani with the ransom money."

The Wrighties said, in their deepest FBI voices, "Case solved."

It's not that Lucy didn't like computers; it's just that the words "handwriting sample" made her pulse speed up. Computers were useful, but it was in good, old-fashioned, everyday handwriting that she could find secret codes and confidential information. Lucy believed that you never knew who someone really was until you saw their handwriting.

"Okay, I'll go to school," she huffed. "But I'm only doing it for the writing samples."

She walked into her room and looked at the stack of boxes that still needed to be unpacked. Her life would be a lot easier if her mom didn't know her so well and her dad didn't wake up so early and she didn't have to go to a new school in a new city. She picked up the backpack that her parents had bought for her new "adventure"—which was another word she could do without—and walked over to her window. The pigeon from last night was still on the windowsill, or maybe this was a different pigeon. *Well,* thought Lucy, *at least someone wants to be here.*

7:50 a.m.
Apartment 7D

"I'm leaving in ten minutes. Are you coming with me?" asked Stella.

"I don't need to go with you. You don't even go to my school anymore," said Nicky. He walked to the cupboard and pulled out a box of cereal.

"Suit yourself. I thought maybe you'd want someone to walk you to school, but it's your life."

Nicky grabbed the milk from the fridge. "Does Dad know you look like that?"

"Like what?" asked Stella.

"You know, like that." He pointed to her face. Nicky figured his sister was trying to look all high-schooly, now that she was a freshman. She had thick black lines under her eyes, her lips were smeared with pumpkin-colored lipstick, and her hair had gone from naturally curly and brown with blond streaks to unnaturally straight and blond with purple streaks.

"If you're not coming with me, I'm leaving. Don't forget to put away the milk and put your bowl in the dishwasher," said Stella.

"I know," said Nicky. "I'm not a baby. You don't always have to tell me what to do."

"Fine. I'll never tell you anything again."

Nicky shoveled six heaping spoonfuls of cereal into his mouth, then stuck his hand into the cereal box.

"What are you doing? You just contaminated the entire box of cereal with your disgusting germs!"

"I don't have germs and if I do, they're king, not disgusting."

"What? Ugh. If you had any friends, you'd know the word is 'awesome,' not 'king.' Nobody says 'That's king.' Nobody even knows what that means." Stella bit down so hard that her head started to shake. She talked through clenched teeth. "Words that pop into my mind to describe your squalid germs include 'revolting' and 'offensive.' Not 'awesome.' And definitely not 'king'!"

"They're king. They're king. They're king." Nicky charged out of the room holding a handful of cereal. "My germs are king. By the way, I beat you out," he taunted.

Stella hollered, "Hey, you didn't put your stuff away like I told you to!"

Nicky slipped into his bedroom and carefully placed the cereal he was holding on his windowsill.

"I don't know where you are," he said out loud to the air, "but here's some breakfast. I sure hope you get to fly fast today."

Stella was still yelling in the kitchen. Nicky tried tuning her out. His ears were too efficient, though. If they weren't so good at doing their job, he wouldn't hear her, and if he didn't hear her, he wouldn't have to remember to go back to the kitchen and put his bowl in the dishwasher and the milk in the fridge. It wasn't his fault that his hearing was so good; he could have been born deaf, and if he had been, he wouldn't have heard his sister. Since that was the case, he decided that it wasn't fair for him to have to go all the way back into the kitchen to clean up simply because of his excellent hearing.

He walked down a long narrow dimly lit hallway.

His father's bedroom and office were on one end of their dog-bone-shaped apartment; everything else was at the other end. Nicky had a hunch that the rooms at his father's end of the apartment were trying to break away from the rest of the rooms and form their own apartment nation. Soon, he figured, he'd probably need a passport to cross into his father's side.

Nicky knocked on the bedroom door. "I'm going to school now," he said.

"Try to behave," his father called out from inside his room.

Then his sister's voice came at him all the way from the kitchen, "Get back in here!"

"Bye, Dad," said Nicky. "It's the first day of school."

He hoped his father's door would swing open and he'd come out of his room, give Nicky a pat on the back, and say something like, "I bet you'll have a great day," or "Good luck."

Instead he got his sister again, "Nicky, I'm not kidding. Get in here. NOW!"

8:00 a.m.

Nicky forgot to press the L button. The elevator started moving as soon as the door closed, so it was easy enough to forget. The elevator lurched to a stop, and the door opened on the sixth floor. In walked an unfamiliar-looking man and a girl with giant eyes and long black hair.

"Good morning," said the man. "We're going down. Mind if I press the button? You see, we're running extremely late, and today's my first day on the job. Another morning I'd enjoy spending some quality time in the elevator, but today we've got to get to the lobby."

Lucy groaned.

Nicky looked at the chrome panel with two rows of buttons. He glanced back over at the girl. He couldn't tell if she was mad or sad or thinking that he was stupid for forgetting to press the button.

"I can do it," he said. Then he blurted out, "I think I live above you. I mean, if you moved into apartment 6D, then I know I live above you. And guess what? Your apartment is shaped the same as ours. Every single apartment on the D-line is. If I dug a hole in the floor of my kitchen, I could jump down and land in your kitchen. That would be king. My bedroom is the one that's across from the kitchen. My sister's got the small room next to the kitchen."

Nicky pressed the L and held his finger on the button until they passed the fourth floor. When they got to the third floor, he tensed up.

"Oh, no. I forgot my backpack. I've got to go back upstairs." He reached out and pressed the seven button and then looked down and noticed he had forgotten to tie his shoelaces too.

Ask Lucy what she thought of her new home and she'd say the only *great* thing that had come out of the move was her room. It had plenty of space for her 216 pens—which included calligraphy, quill, ballpoint, fountain, and felt-tip pens—fourteen books about handwriting; two microscopes; a desk long enough for a twenty-two-inch light box, computer, and scanner; four filing cabinets, and enough shelves for 112 different brands and textures of paper, forensic powders, and liquid solutions

Nothing else was really working out. She had come to the conclusion that the boy with the floppy orange hair and untied shoelaces that she had seen in the elevator had made it his life's mission to annoy her. His bedroom seemed to be directly above Lucy's, and he did jumping jacks, or some sort of jump-roll-thumping-on-the-floor activity, almost every afternoon, all afternoon, and into the night. What had she ever done to deserve this?

It sure would have been nice to get a sample of his handwriting. She wanted to see what clues she could find that would help her understand what made him do all that jumping, thumping, and pounding. She wished she had asked him for a handwriting sample back on Monday morning, but you can't just blurt out "So I'm wondering if I can have some of your handwriting?" to a random boy in the elevator.

As for school, she'd describe the week with one word: *disastrous*. Since her mother had told her to, she had asked all the kids in her class for handwriting samples. Pigtailed and purse-lipped Robin Miller had refused the request first. "My writing is my business, and you're an outsider. No one will give you their writing. I'll make sure of that," she'd told Lucy.

Almost all the others had followed suit. "My writing is my business, and you're an outsider." They'd said it over and over again. Exact words, just as though Robin Miller had recorded them onto their brains. Lucy couldn't believe it. Weren't the kids here taught to be nice to the new girl?

Okay, a few brave kids who didn't seem to care about Robin Miller, or any of the repercussions that might come to them for disobeying one of her absurd edicts, gave Lucy writing samples. Lucy pasted those samples into the handwriting analysis journal that her classmates in Savannah had given her.

No matter what happened, she knew she'd stay away from Brad Miller, Robin's twin brother. His writing had sharp and dark lines, like he'd rather use his pen for stabbing than for writing. This was a bad sign if ever there were one. The Wrighties would have suggested taking drastic action. Transfer schools. Get on a bus. Leave the city. Letters shouldn't look like knives, guns, spears, or daggers. If they did, watch out, because something terrible could happen. Lucy sighed and said to herself, "It looks like I better keep in mind LWR number one."

September 2

Brad Miller

Why are you here?

Caroline Minty and her handwriting seemed confused. Caroline couldn't decide what she wanted to eat, what she wanted to do, or even what her voice should sound like. Sometimes she spoke really loudly, sometimes she had a French accent, and sometimes she spoke so quietly that you had to position your ear directly in front of her mouth to hear her. Her handwriting was both large and small and slanted to the left as well as the right. In took her until Friday before she decided to give Lucy some of her handwriting. As soon as she handed it to her, she asked for it back. Then she changed her mind and said, "Actually, you can keep it."

September 4

Caroline Minty

Maybe we can be friends

Bazzy Milo had big round handwriting that looked like big round Bazzy, and Jupiter Howell had itty-bitty tiny handwriting, just like itty-bitty tiny Jupiter. Latoya Davis's handwriting looked friendly, honest and sophisticated. It wasn't too big or too small and wasn't filled with curlicues, which meant that she didn't always need to be the center of attention. Her letters were fully formed. The tops of her *f*s, *h*s and *l*s popped up over the line a little higher than they should, but that just meant Latoya liked to think about things before doing them. Lucy hoped they'd become friends. (Unfortunately, Latoya Davis changed schools before the end of the month to get away from the Miller twins. Lucy got the feeling from Latoya's handwriting that the decision to switch schools was well thought out.)

It was finally Friday afternoon, and Lucy had two full days ahead of her to repack all the boxes she had spent the week unpacking, and convince her parents that things weren't working out and it was time to move back to Savannah. Lucy looked out her bedroom window and saw a pigeon resting on the ledge again. She had a weird feeling it had been watching her. She walked over to her desk and picked up a magnifying glass and a copy of a postcard with Amelia Earhart's signature on it. She started to examine it but couldn't get her mind off the pigeon. She looked back at her window. The pigeon seemed to wink at her. She pulled a toothpick out of her desk drawer and carefully traced the signature with it. She glanced at her window. The pigeon bobbed its head forward and then bowed, like it was gesturing hello. Lucy looked back down at the signature. She turned it upside down. She pulled her hair back into a ponytail and tried to focus on the details of the lines but couldn't. She turned her head. The pigeon was definitely watching her.

"You know," Lucy said, "Amelia Earhart probably wished she were a pigeon. She signed her name vertically, instead of across the page, like she wanted to launch herself into the air. She loved to fly."

The pigeon nodded as if in agreement and then, to Lucy's surprise, spoke, "Yes, I've heard that."

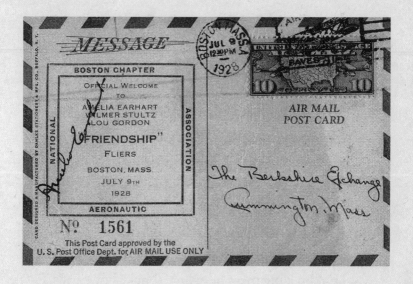

4:00 p.m.
Apartment 8G

Nicky tapped his foot on Grandma Zelda's kitchen floor and told her about the three new tall girls in his class. They were different girls from the tall girl who'd just moved into his building. That girl probably went to another school. On the morning when he'd met her in the elevator, she and her dad had turned right and crossed the street at the corner where Nicky had taken a left. That was fine; he didn't need a fourth tall girl looming over him.

Nicky hadn't grown in two years. After his mother had moved to India, he'd stopped growing. It was like his body had decided to stay the same height until she came home, only two years later she still hadn't returned, which meant that Nicky was the same size as most nine-year-olds and the shortest kid in his class.

Grandma Zelda cut three slices of savory Zeldaberry pie. She served one to Nicky, put another slice on the table next to him, and set the third slice outside the window on the windowsill. She settled herself into the chair next to Nicky.

"Eat up a big mess of my pie, Nicky honey. It's a sure thing for growth spurts. I remember the summer your papa and I moved to Dayton. The boy grew a heap that August, and when he started at his new school, not one person believed he was ten years old. They stuck him in the eighth grade. Imagine that, a ten-year-old."

"What happened?" asked Nicky.

"No one had any horse sense back then. You'd think they'd listen to the boy's mother. But, no. They insisted we were thievin' with the truth."

"Is that why Dad graduated from high school when he was fourteen?"

"I'm afraid so," sighed Grandma Zelda. She looked down at her hands, which had a slight tremor, and closed her eyes. Grandma Zelda was known to take short naps. Some of her naps could fit between two sentences. When her eyes reopened, sixty-seven seconds after she had closed them, she asked, "How's he behaving these days? I haven't heard a peep out of him in weeks."

"He snarled yesterday," replied Nicky. "It's better than the yelling but not as king as talking."

Grandma Zelda shook her head and brushed a pile of Zeldaberry pie crumbs off the table. "I remember once . . ." Nicky finished his pie, stood up, even though Grandma Zelda was in the middle of a story, and walked to the open window. "I haven't gotten into trouble once this week," he whispered to a pigeon. "I think things are going to be a lot better this year."

PART THREE

SEVEN MONTHS LATER

WEDNESDAY, MARCH 31
4:55 p.m.
West 68th Street, Apartment 7D

Nicky stretched his arms out wide. He lifted them up and pushed them down, slowly at first and then faster. He jumped. He landed.

"Drat," he said, and got back onto the bed.

This time he started fast and slowed down. He jumped. He landed.

He got back on the bed and tried again.

5:00 p.m.
Apartment 6D

Dear Everyone,

The handwriting journal you gave me is full! It actually took a lot longer to fill it up than I thought it would. People in Savannah are much nicer about giving you samples of their handwriting than they are here. Everyone is so busy all the time, they don't even have time left

over to pick up a pen. I'm not
kidding! And when they do write,
you wouldn't believe how messy
their handwriting can be. I can't
wait to move back home.

Love,

Your friend and former
classmate, Lucy

Lucy hadn't written to anyone at her old school
since December. Thinking about her new life was
bad enough; she couldn't bear to write people from
home about it. What would she say? *Dear Everyone,
How are you? I'm not fine. I've never been this not fine
before. Please come kidnap me and bring me back to
Savannah.* No need to send that kind of letter, she
thought, so she simply stopped writing.

At her new school it wasn't enough to have a
best friend. You were supposed to have a best
friend forever. Lucy despised BFFs. Just look at the
way most kids wrote the letters *BFF,* and you knew
the whole thing could end any minute. If you really

wanted a BFF, you had better show some commitment with your letters. Lucy would never pick a BFF who didn't have BFF handwriting. Caroline Minty had asked Lucy to be her BFF in November, but Caroline Minty had the least BFFy handwriting Lucy had ever seen, so Lucy'd had to tell her no.

LWR #3: REAL FRIENDS WRITE WITH REAL LETTERS.

Who wants to think about forever when you're eleven, anyway? Lucy wondered if any of those BFFs out there really took the time to sit down and think about what it meant before they all started BFFing each other. If you BFF someone when you're eleven, you might as well get married, and you don't see a lot of eleven-year-olds getting married. *There's a good reason for that,* thought Lucy.

That whole BFF thing wasn't even the worst of it. Sure, Lucy had known to be careful since the first time she'd glimpsed the terrible Miller twins' handwriting. On that day in December when Robin Miller gave Mrs. Costa a note supposedly from her mother, Lucy realized it would be safer not to say anything. After Mrs. Costa had dropped the note, and it had slid under Lucy's chair. Lucy considered picking it up and handing it directly to Mrs. Costa. She hadn't had the willpower, though. She had to read the note first. Then she had to open her mouth.

Dear Mrs. Costa,

We've had a terrible family emergency. I'd like to tell you how bad it was, but it's too terrible to talk about. Robin and Brad are tramatized and will not be able to do any homework this month. It's a miracle that they can even come to school.

Sincerely Yours,

Mrs. Nicole Miller

"Robin wrote this, not her mom," Lucy said before giving the note back to Mrs. Costa.

"Excuse me," said Mrs. Costa.

"I thought you'd want to know," said Lucy.

"She's used a vocabulary word but spelled it wrong. See, that's not how you spell 'traumatized.' Also, her letters are too dark. If Mrs. Miller really wrote that note, she wouldn't be pushing her pen down on the paper like that; she'd be writing quickly. You might even see gaps in her letters."

Lucy thought she was doing Mrs. Costa a favor; Mrs. Costa thought otherwise. She yelled at Lucy for reading a note that wasn't intended for her. After class Robin and Brad Miller proclaimed Lucy public enemy number one. "We're holding a ceremony after school to make it official. Come if you dare," Robin told Lucy.

When you're public enemy number one, it means someone's going to try to trip you in the hallway at least once a day and that people will be whispering about you in whispers so loud that the only thing whispery about them is that they are hidden behind a hand. It also means your days of getting handwriting samples are done with.

Since the day of the note, Caroline Minty was the only kid in her class who still talked to her—on some days, at least. She'd decide to talk to Lucy, then figure she better not, then refigure and talk to Lucy again.

Sixth grade was three-quarters done, and Lucy had made one part-time friend. There was no way she could tell people back in Savannah that the person she spent the most time talking to wasn't even a person. They'd think she'd gone stark-raving loony. Who knows, she thought, maybe she had.

Lucy walked over to her window and looked out of it. "Pigeon," she called out. "Where are you?" Then she looked up, not at the sky but at her ceiling and wondered if the thumping would ever end.

"Pigeon," Lucy called out again. "I have an important question to ask you."

5:05 p.m.
Upper West Side

Pigeon leisurely flew down Amsterdam Avenue. The buildings shimmered in the sun, as if someone had walked around the neighborhood with a can of sparkly orange spray paint, and the emerald-green feathers around Pigeon's neck flickered like real gems. March had been an unusually warm month, which meant that the birds in the city had been making quite a ruckus, celebrating a bounty of worms and food droppings. Pigeon had recently conducted a survey and found that one out of five people walking and eating at the same time dropped some portion of their food. The number increased to one in three if the people were under the age of twelve. Not that she cared. She didn't need street scraps. She had Grandma Zelda, and that meant all the Zeldaberry pie she could possibly eat.

Pigeon had become a close personal confidant of three people who lived in Lucy's building on West Sixty-eighth Street: Lucy Bertel, who'd moved into apartment 6D in September; Nicky Gibson, whose habit of getting in trouble had kept him in his bedroom in apartment 7D; and Nicky's grandma Zelda, who hadn't left apartment 8G since Pigeon had met her. (Honestly, it's not that odd for a pigeon to have human friends. Humans have a long renowned history of caring for, working with, and sharing secrets with pigeons.)

Pigeon didn't have a particularly soothing or

melodious voice. She wasn't mind-bogglingly brilliant, nor was she dazzlingly beautiful. She enjoyed a good meal and a well-told story, and while she made it perfectly clear that she wasn't fond of everyone, she stayed devoted to those whom she felt needed her companionship. Her gift was loyalty.

Pigeon spent quite a bit of her leisure time conducting surveys. She had recently counted the number of sparrows, mice, and rats on five city streets during the hour between eleven a.m. and noon. The sparrows outnumbered the mice and rats on three of the streets. One street had no sparrows—it was about time, thought Pigeon—and one rat. One street was entirely empty. Next week she planned on returning to the same five streets at the same time. It would be nice to find an actual city block that hadn't been invaded by sparrows.

On squintingly sunny days, like today, Grandma Zelda's kitchen window remained open, thankfully. Because when it was closed, Pigeon couldn't see a thing through it. Thick layers of grease and grime coated the glass. It made the world inside turn into a smudgy blur. Pigeon complained to Grandma

Zelda about her windows, but it didn't make one bit of difference.

The truth was that Nicky's grandma Zelda hadn't cleaned a window in decades. She would be the first one to admit that getting old had advantages and disadvantages, and dirty windows were one of the disadvantages. Some of the other disadvantages, included misplacing your teeth (dentures), misplacing your ears (hearing aids), misplacing your eyes (glasses), and essentially misplacing anything that you put down and then later decided you wanted to pick up again. Grandma Zelda sometimes spent as many as four hours a day looking for things. Sometimes her search so exhausted her that she'd take a nap. When she awoke, she could no longer remember what she had been looking for, which was one of the advantages of getting old. Something is no longer lost if you don't remember you're looking for it.

Pigeon touched down and let out a symphonic-sounding coo. She hit her high note, and her pitch was spot-on. Hopefully Grandma Zelda caught it. The one thing Grandma Zelda could always hear was music. Somehow her ears never went deaf when it came to the sound of music. Grandma Zelda had once told Pigeon, "Plato believed music gave wings to the mind, flight to the imagination, and charm and gaiety to life." She went on to say, "Now, of course Plato didn't tell this to me himself. Even though I'm old, I'm strictly AD. Sadly, I missed out on those rollicking BC times. I'd surely have enjoyed them." Pigeon didn't know who Plato was, but she liked people who understood that having wings was a good thing.

Pigeon triple-bobbed her head and ruffled her rump before letting out another coo, this one, unfortunately, off-key. She looked inside Grandma Zelda's kitchen and saw a most unpleasant, and truly unexpected, sight.

5:12 p.m.
West 68th Street, Apartment 8G

Peter Reginald Gibson's long knobby fingers were wrapped around Grandma Zelda's frail shoulder. Not affectionately, mind you. It looked like a good-for-nothing mean-spirited grip.

Peter Reginald Gibson was a tall man with a rotund midsection that magically managed to balance itself on a pair of spindly legs, and as if that weren't enough to call him odd-looking, he often had what appeared to be a spider's web of sleep gunk under his left eye. Mr. Gibson's voice had a deep, booming quality. When he talked, it sounded like he was using a microphone. Grown-ups described his voice as *commanding*; kids called it *scary*. Because of this thunderously loud voice, it seemed like he spoke a lot more than he actually did. In reality Mr. Gibson was a man of few, mostly unpleasant, words. In addition to all this, during the past few years he had started balding, and with each strand of graying hair that fell off his head, he seemed to get nastier.

(The connection between the two seemed so obvious to Nicky that he told his science teacher he wanted to measure the correlation between bad mood growth and hair loss for his sixth-grade science fair project. He even offered to bring his father to school and keep him locked in the classroom for a few weeks, so they could study him. His teacher recommended he come up with an alternative idea, something more along the lines of measuring mold growth on different types of bread.)

Mr. Gibson released Grandma Zelda with a flick of the wrist that sent her spinning around like a dog in hot pursuit of her tail. She whirled across the kitchen, past the stove and the fridge, slowing down and finally collapsing onto a rickety chair.

Pigeon could see Grandma Zelda's sky-blue eyes through her closed lids. *He's no better than a sparrow,* she thought. She pushed her wings back and prepared to—then quickly stopped herself from flying inside to save Grandma Zelda, or peck at Mr. Gibson, or both. *Stay calm, and no matter what happens,* she reminded herself, *don't break through the invisible wall.*

"Can you hear me, Mother?" Mr. Gibson pointed to an x: _____ at the bottom of a long piece of paper. "Sign here!"

Grandma Zelda's eyelids lifted and she started to read. Her head moved from left to right, as if the words started on one side of the room and stretched sheer across to the other side. "Well, darlin', doesn't this just take the fruitcake," she said.

Grandma Zelda rarely got frazzled. She had witnessed a lot in her long life, enough to keep her aging nerves calm. During her many years on this planet, she had survived a tsunami; walked across Kansas; won a dog sled race in Antarctica; gotten married to a man who'd turned out to be a thief and a scoundrel—and those were his good traits; had her only child a week before her fiftieth birthday, which was a bit of a shock to everyone; gotten divorced; lived in a bus; played her viola d'amore (which is like a violin with extra strings) every single day until it got stolen; had the viola d'amore returned by the thief's wife; befriended the wife after a reporter wrote a story about the incident; become famous, and performed a concert for a prince. That's not all, but there's not enough space left in that sentence to keep going.

Mr. Gibson kept the tip of his long finger attached to the x:_____. He stuffed a pen into Grandma Zelda's hand. "Sign here," he said again.

Grandma Zelda dropped the pen onto the floor.

Mr. Gibson picked it up and pushed it into the palm of Grandma Zelda's hand.

"Oh, my. Heavens to Betsy," she said, and flinched.

Pigeon pecked at the air and reminded herself about the invisible wall for the second time.

Mr. Gibson placed his large hand over Grandma Zelda's delicate one and gobbled it up in a fist sandwich. Then he picked up their combined hands and moved them to the x:_____. He guided the pen over the line, but it escaped his control and he hollered. (It actually may have been his normal talking voice; it's difficult to decipher one from the other with him.)

"THIS IS A SCRIBBLE, A SCRAWL. NOT A SIGNATURE."

Grandma Zelda adjusted her glasses and looked closely at the page. "Yes, I do see what you mean." Then she launched into one of her stories, "Dear, did I ever tell you about the time I won the Montana state vocabulary bee by knowing the definition of the word 'cacography'? We were knee deep into it, round twenty-six. 'Cacography.' Mind you, it's not a word most children feel eager to repeat in front of a room full of bored people. The definition, if you don't know, is 'poor penmanship,' like we see a stunning example of right here."

Mr. Gibson didn't say another word. He walked out of the kitchen. His huffing breath trailed along a foot or two behind him.

"Are you leaving now?" asked Grandma Zelda. "Would you like some pie before you go? I've got one that's ready to come out of the oven."

Yes, thought Pigeon from her perch. It was just like Grandma Zelda to offer pie even when she was being told to do something she didn't want to do. She'd feed anyone, even her worst enemy. Grandma Zelda would probably say, "Enemies get hungry too."

Not Pigeon, though. She'd never feed her enemies. She had other plans for them, and particularly for Mr. Gibson. She vowed, right then and there, that someday she'd get him back. Yes, she would, right smack in the middle of his head.

5:20 p.m.

"Are you hurt?" asked Pigeon.

"Oh, no, dear. I'm fit as a fiddle," said Grandma Zelda. She smiled. "My son's a bit bowed up, that's all." She picked up the pen and shuffled around some papers on the table. Then she curled her back like a snail and started writing. After several minutes, she slowly stood up. Of course slowly. Grandma Zelda did everything slowly these days.

She held out the piece of paper toward Pigeon.

"I'd like you to deliver this note to Nicky for me."

Pigeon glared at what now looked like a poisonous weed sprouting out of Grandma Zelda's hand and shook her head. "I'm not trained as a carrier pigeon. I can't. I won't. I'll crash. My feathers will fall out. Carrier pigeons are strong and mighty. They have personal trainers who were world champion heavyweight boxers. I've heard that carrier pigeons are born with a special magnet stuck in them. I don't have a magnet in me. I just have me in me, and there's not a whole lot of me in there."

Grandma Zelda smiled and winked at Pigeon. She didn't need to use words to make her case. Little gestures did enough. She placed one hand over her wrinkled cheek.

Pigeon looked away. She'd never be able to say no to Grandma Zelda if she looked at her. "I can't help you with this. Oh, look. It's the sun. I can barely see it. Sun is setting. I better go. You know what I mean."

She opened her wings and hopped off the windowsill, coasting for a few seconds before flapping.

Pigeon peered through a smudge on the glass. She moved three inches to the left and looked through another smudge. She hopped another two inches leftward. Did anyone in Nicky's family ever clean their windows? Through this third smudge she could make out a moving blob.

She tapped twice on the glass. The blob lengthened. She tapped again, this time ten pecks in quick succession. The blob oozed over to the window and opened it.

"You scared me," said Nicky (blob turns into boy).

"Are you in time-out?" asked Pigeon.

Nicky turned his head and looked at the door to his room. Once convinced he was safely alone, he turned his head back toward the window and whispered, "It wasn't my fault. I was holding the ball and it jumped out of my hand. I didn't throw it. Well, not exactly. I kind of helped it jump, but I didn't mean for it to bounce up and land on the table. I really didn't mean for it to break a glass. Do you believe me, Pigeon?"

"Are you telling me the truth? I always believe

you when you say you're telling me the truth."

"Mostly," admitted Nicky. "I'm telling you most of the truth. I'm keeping some of the truth for myself, at least for now."

"Fair enough," said Pigeon. "Let me know when you want to tell me the rest of the truth."

"I'm bored. I'm supposed to stay in my room all afternoon. My dad won't even let me go upstairs to see Grandma Zelda," groaned Nicky.

"That's because he was up there with her, and you wouldn't believe what—" Pigeon paused. Sometimes her words barreled out of her beak before her brain had time to figure out how they would affect the person she was talking to. This time, for once, her brain stopped her in time—barely. Perhaps she shouldn't tell Nicky about what she had seen. She'd save some of the truth for later too. "Your grandmother wrote a note. She wanted me to deliver it to you."

"That's king. Where is it?" asked Nicky.

"Um, she has it," said Pigeon. She paused before adding, "I have an idea. Why don't I teach you how to fly and you can go get it yourself? Your dad will never know you've left your room."

Nicky looked at the metal protective grate that spanned the length of his window. It separated those who could fly from those who couldn't, a not-so-subtle reminder that humans do not have wings. Nicky spent most of his days and nights jumping off his bed and flapping his arms, hoping that just once, and then a thousand more times, he'd catch the air and take flight. He didn't need this reminder.

"I wish you could teach me," said Nicky. "I don't see why it's so easy for you. No offense, but you don't look like you should be able to fly, but you can, and I've tried everything I can think of, and I still can't. Flapping my towel didn't work, neither did my sheets. I cut a hole in my pillow and glued the feathers onto my arms. That didn't work either. What's your trick?"

Pigeon eyed Nicky up and down. "It is a chirping shame you have those arms. I suppose you have airplanes to make up for them. Although I don't understand why anyone would want to be in the air sitting in an oversize sausage. Don't worry about the note. I'm sure it's not important. She just wrote it because your dad was shaking her and trying to force her to sign that piece of paper." Oh, dear.

Mouth bypassed brain. Not good. Pigeon swiveled her neck around. She didn't want to see Nicky's expression. She scanned the tops of the neighboring town houses. She spotted a sliver of the river and changed the subject. "When did you say you were sailing around the world? That sounds like fun."

"When I'm eighteen," said Nicky. "What was my dad doing to Grandma Zelda?"

"How long do you think the trip will take?" Pigeon asked.

"A year. What was my dad doing to Grandma Zelda?" repeated Nicky.

"Your dad?" asked Pigeon, stalling.

"Yes," replied Nicky.

"You mean your dad," she confirmed.

"Yes," he said again. "Pigeon, what's going on?"

"Did you know sailing is like flying over water? I once took a survey to see which birds like to swim over the water and which ones prefer land. Would you be interested in hearing what I found out?"

"Stop trying to change the subject," said Nicky, "and tell me what my dad was doing."

"I don't know if I should tell you. It's upsetting, and I don't want you to be sad. You know, your grandma has told me stories about some of the things your father has done, and they're not terribly nice. But not everything he's done is bad. He had you, didn't he? That was good. Better than good," said Pigeon.

"Pigeon, do you know if my dad's done anything really bad?" Nicky long held out hope that his father might be a secret superhero, grumpy to the outside world so that no one suspected he was saving innocent people from bad guys. It made for the perfect cover. Mr. Gibson worked from home, so he could come and go whenever he wanted. Since he pretty much snapped at everyone he spoke to, no one would guess he cared about helping people in trouble. Clark Kent was already mild-mannered and nice. Everybody at the *Daily Planet* should have figured out he was Superman. It was pretty obvious. And weren't they reporters, anyway? The *Daily Planet* must have been a pretty bad newspaper if no one could even figure out that Superman was working there.

"Sometimes your father acts positively sparrow-like," sighed Pigeon.

Mr. Gibson hadn't been snarly and scary forever. Back before Nicky's mom moved to India,

Nicky's TOA was only about .025. Nicky sort of remembered going to a Mets game with his father and playing Frisbee in the park. Now, though, Mr. Gibson stayed in his office on one side of the apartment and kept Nicky in his room on the other side. In a weird way that almost made things better. Spending any time with his father these days gave Nicky an acute case of the clumsies. He'd drop something and break it. Or he'd trip over things and break them. Or he'd do something that ended up with some breakable thing splintering into pieces. Then he'd get yelled at and put in another time-out. At which point Nicky would throw something against the wall, and one more thing would end up broken.

Of course, if Nicky's father were a superhero, then all the time-outs would be worth it. They wouldn't even feel like time-outs anymore. If his dad was just another bad guy, then Nicky had wasted his entire childhood.

"Call your grandmother. Ask her about your dad and the note," suggested Pigeon.

"I'll get in bigger trouble if my dad finds me on the phone. Remember how mad he got after I accidentally dropped the phone in the toilet? Well, after a piece of gum got stuck to the other phone and somehow ended up in Stella's hair, I got banned from using the phone until I'm eighteen and too old to even want to use a phone. Why did Grandma Zelda write me a note?" asked Nicky.

"Probably just to say hello. Nothing important," said Pigeon.

"I bet it is important. Why'd she write it if it wasn't important?" asked Nicky.

"You know your grandmother," said Pigeon. "She does lots of things that aren't important."

"She doesn't write notes that aren't important, though," Nicky responded.

"Yes, she does. All the time. She's always writing unimportant notes." Pigeon was getting agitated.

"Every note I've seen her write has been important," Nicky said.

"How many notes have you seen her write?" asked Pigeon.

"I don't know. Probably a thousand."

"Well, I've seen her write twice that many, and none of them has been important." Once again Pigeon had lost total control of the words coming out of her beak. She didn't mean to lie. She only meant to win her point. If only she could remember what that point was.

"What did you say my dad was doing to her?"

Oh, no. Not again. Pigeon felt like she was on a migratory flight that she wanted to get off. She'd make Nicky an offer that she hoped he'd refuse. "Maybe I should get the note for you. Do you want me to fly upstairs, all the way around to the back of the building, where for all I know it's possible a hawk is lurking, to get you the note?" asked Pigeon.

"Yes," Nicky said.

"I may be risking life and wing to do it," she added.

"What do you mean?" asked Nicky. "Pigeons are supposed to carry notes."

"Not all pigeons," replied Pigeon. "Some of us are just here to be friendly." She bowed down.

"Well, I think you're a note pigeon," said Nicky. "Anyway, you're the one who offered."

If Grandma Zelda were here, she would tell Pigeon that she had sure opened a can of worms. Until this moment Pigeon hadn't understood how opening a can of worms could ever be a bad thing.

Pigeon stretched out her neck, but not so far that her beak crossed the invisible wall. (Pigeon knew that many humans had issues with pigeons. Although she believed these to be irrational and insulting, she took precautions nevertheless and stayed on her side of the window. She never ever flew inside an apartment. Rarely did she even poke her head in. It's true that Grandma Zelda, Nicky, and Lucy had all invited her inside. When they did, she told each of them the same thing, "Please don't expect me to come in, and please don't ask me again. I have one rule that I live by. *Remain on the outside of the invisible wall.*" Lucy respected Pigeon's wish and had never asked her to come into her room again. Grandma Zelda often told Pigeon to stop being such a stranger and come on in. Pigeon would remind Grandma Zelda of her rule, and Grandma Zelda would respond by saying, "Gracious, how could I have forgotten that?" Nicky forgot too, or just didn't care. "Come on, just once," he'd say. "No. No. No," Pigeon would reply.)

She saw Grandma Zelda at the kitchen table with her eyes closed. Her right arm moved back and forth in front of her left shoulder, while her left arm dangled down by her side. After she finished playing Beethoven's *Moonlight Sonata* on her air viola d'amore, she opened her eyes.

"Well, hello there." She sounded surprised. Grandma Zelda often sounded excited, even amazed, when Pigeon visited, as if she were seeing a long-lost friend, instead of the same pigeon that stopped by almost every day. "Have you come for some Zeldaberry pie?"

"No," replied Pigeon. "I'm here for Nicky's note."

Grandma Zelda stared at Pigeon for a good long stretch of time. She recalled something about a note, but it took her a while to remember what she had written on it. Once she got that sorted out in her head, all she needed to do was figure out where she had put it.

6:12 p.m.

The principals of flying, as Pigeon knew them, no longer applied. She recalculated for wind drifts and additional weight, but when a wind snap came at her from below and sent Grandma Zelda's note flapping over her face, she found herself soaring blind, and nothing had prepared her for that. There are no Seeing Eye dogs for birds; you have no choice but to fly blind if you can't see. Fly, spiral—it was hard to tell what she was doing. She plunged down, then up to the left. The note flipped back over, and she could see again.

This on-the-job training is not for the birds, thought Pigeon. If she was going to be a carrier pigeon she wanted to study with a professional. Arghhh.

Up. Down. Across, across, across.

                              Up.

                    Up.

        UP.

Back, back, back, back.

                              Down.

                              Down.

Wings drooping and getting tired.
Down.

Across, across, across, across, across, across, across, across, across.

Sputter to a stop.

Crash landing. She teetered on Nicky's windowsill, the note successfully carried from Grandma Zelda's window to Nicky's. Pigeon would be the first in line to admit that she was certifiably NOT a carrier pigeon and swore to herself that this would be the first and forever last note she ever delivered.

She stared through a handprint on Nicky's window. His room looked empty, escaped-hamster cage empty. Infuriatingly empty. And why had he closed his window when he knew she was coming back with the note? Sometimes that boy had the brain of a sparrow. She gasped for breath and reasoned with herself. Nicky spent practically all his time in his room. Surely the chance that he'd return in mere seconds was close to 100 percent. When her shadow shifted a notch to the left, she downgraded to 99 percent.

94 percent.

75 percent.

50 percent.

38 percent.

Really? How could this be?

Pigeon turned to look at the sky and noticed a cloud pressing up against the setting sun. When she turned back, she saw that Nicky's room remained as empty as a bear's lair in June.

22 percent.

14 percent.

The probability that Nicky would soon walk into his room had dwindled down to 2 percent. Pigeon thought about flying back around the apartment building and returning the note to Grandma Zelda. She also considered opening her beak and letting it float away, but that option stunk like a sparrow too. Even though she was not—repeat, NOT—a carrier pigeon, and swore that she would NEVER be a carrier pigeon, she believed it was her duty as a pigeon, and a friend, to get this note to Nicky, or at least for Grandma Zelda to believe she had. *Yes,* Pigeon figured, *at this point, that was good enough.* That's when she decided to give the note to Lucy.

6:23 p.m.

"This is better than finding a note in a bottle," squealed a delighted Lucy.

"It's not for you," said Pigeon.

"Of course it is," said Lucy. "Just look at this hand-writing. I can't wait to analyze it. You don't see writing like this much anymore. Who gave this to you?"

"Zelda."

"Oh, yeah," Lucy looked at the name on the note. "I knew that."

"It's for Nicky, the boy upstairs. That's her grandson," explained Pigeon.

"Oh, Pigeon. You know I'll appreciate this more than that thumping, jumping, ceiling-rattling head-banger. He'd probably just lose it; I will study it carefully. A boy like that isn't worthy of writing like this. "You're a fantastic friend to give this to me."

"No, I'm not," said Pigeon. "It's not for you. It's just for you for now."

"Whatever you say," said Lucy. Consumed by the swirl and tilt of the letters, Lucy didn't realize she had started repeating herself. "You're a fantastic friend. You're a fantastic friend."

Her head popped up, "Look at this *I*," she said. She held the note up for Pigeon to see and pointed to an *I*. "Pigeon, I've been meaning to ask you an important question."

"What is it?" said Pigeon.

"What do you think about the letter *I*?"

"Is that the question?" asked Pigeon, clearly confused.

"Of course," said Lucy. "Well?"

Pigeon bobbed her head and carefully considered, for the first time, the letter *I*. She felt a tad reluctant to admit that she didn't think about a lot of important things, like the letter *I*, even though she hadn't known until now that thinking about the letter *I* was important.

"Since I'm a pigeon, I don't spend much time thinking about letters. I'd rather calculate wingspan and flight schedules than alphabets."

Lucy smiled at Pigeon. "Trust me, you should know about *I*s. They're very meaningful. And I'm not just saying that. You wouldn't believe how much you can tell about a person by the way they write their *I*s. I can tell just by looking at the way she wrote her *I* that I'd like Zelda. I bet that head-stomping grandson of hers has a big disgusting, sloppy *I* though, like he thinks he's the center of the universe and doesn't care that anyone lives below him. If he had a regular *I*, he wouldn't be jumping on top of my head all the time."

LWR #4: You are your *I*.

"No, on second thought," said Lucy, "I bet he has a tiny, barely visible *I* and doesn't think anyone cares about him, so he jumps around all day long to try to get someone to notice him. Well, if that's the case, it's working. I definitely notice him. He needs a bigger *I* immediately. Why do I have to be the one that's forced to notice him? Doesn't he have parents or friends who can pay attention to him?"

Pigeon bobbed her head until every detail of Lucy's face became crisp. "Let's see. His mom flew, on an airplane, to India two years ago and lives there now. I don't even want to tell you about his dad. You'd never believe me anyway. But I will say I'd rather live with a sparrow than with Nicky's father, and if you've ever spent time with a sparrow, you'll know how bad his dad must be for me to say that. I think Nicky gets on his sister's nerves too."

"I can imagine."

"I'm sure his *I*s are fine. He has the best grand-mother ever. She notices him all the time. And he has me, except for right now, because at the moment I'm angry at him and he doesn't have me. But usually he does. What else do you need for a good *I*?"

"If you're convinced he's got such a great and amazing *I*, and I'm sure he has a teensy *I*, let's bet on it and see who's right."

"I'm in."

"Me too," said Lucy. "Fly upstairs and tell him to give us some of his writing so we can see who wins."

"No, you."

"I don't fly."

"Take the elevator, then."

"I don't know him."

"Neither do I."

"What?" Lucy's face shifted positions, and Pigeon lost her focus. "Yes, you do."

Pigeon looked to the left, then looked to the right, then back at Lucy. "I don't like to mix business with family. He's not there anyway. Can't you tell?"

Lucy listened. There was no thumping or pounding or creaking on her ceiling.

"You're right," she said. "It's a miracle. We should celebrate."

"First why don't you tell me what the note I gave you says?"

Lucy began to read Zelda's note. "'My Dearest Nicky, I must—'"

"Honey, dinner is ready." Dr. Bertel's head popped into Lucy's room. "Come along right now, please."

"I'm coming, Mom. Just one second."

"No, honey. It's late."

"One second more, Mom. Just one. I promise."

"Okay, one. There it goes," said Dr. Bertel. "I'm afraid your second is over. Finish up after dinner. It's already past six thirty and I'm not leaving your room without you."

Lucy carefully put down the note and walked out of her room with her mother.

6:38 p.m.

Every night at six thirty Lucy's family ate dinner together. At the table one person thought up an ethical question, and each of the Bertels had to say what they believed would be the right thing to do. Dr. Bertel's questions usually had something to do with medicine, like if two patients come into the hospital at the same time and you're the only doctor there, which person should you treat first—the one who has a minor injury and needs only a few minutes of care or the person who might die if you don't see them right away but will take many hours to treat, meaning the person with the minor injury would have to wait for hours before being seen? Mr. Bertel's questions tended to focus on math. It's amazing how many not funny ethical questions he could make up about math. Like, if seven eight nine, should seven get dessert too? Tonight was Lucy's night to ask a question. It didn't take her long to think of one.

"If someone has a letter that looks like a spear in their signature, should they be put in jail?"

"Is that illegal? I didn't know having a spear in your signature is against the law," said Dr. Bertel.

"It's not," said Lucy. "But I think it should be. Dad, what about you?"

"Hmmm," said Mr. Bertel. "Lucy-loo, this certainly is a tough one. Is it more of a dagger or a trident?"

"Either one," said Lucy.

"Harpoon?"

"Anything like that." Lucy dipped her potato into the ketchup.

Lucy's mother chimed in, "Is that Brad Miller bothering you again?"

"He bothers everyone," replied Lucy. "You should see his *Ls* in the way he writes 'Miller.' I think he should be kicked out of school for those *Ls*. They look like two spears. I don't know why nobody does anything about it."

Mr. Bertel said, "The guidance counselor has talked to him about his behavior. His parents aren't terribly responsive, though. You know there's going to be an assembly soon about bullying."

"That's not going to do anything. I don't think Brad Miller's going to start planting daffodils and giving hugs to five-year-olds if there's an assembly. Why do all teachers think every problem can be solved with an assembly? I'm telling you, Brad Miller should be expelled and put in jail."

"On what grounds?" asked Mr. Bertel. "Coming to school with a hidden spear in his signature?"

"I'm not kidding," said Lucy. She put a spoonful of peas into her mouth and made a face. "It's like John Wilkes Booth. He had a dagger in his signature. If someone had paid some attention to that, maybe they could have stopped him before he assassinated President Lincoln. John Wilkes Booth could have been stopped, and so can Brad Miller."

"Booth had a dagger in his signature?" asked Dr. Bertel.

"Right there for everybody to see. And you know who else did?" Lucy had a feeling she was about to score big points and her parents would soon see her side. "Al Capone."

"The mobster? That Al Capone?" asked Mr. Bertel.

"Yeah, the one who went to Alcatraz, who's in those books I like. I've seen pictures of what his signature looked like before he started shooting people, and I'm telling you his *l* looks just like Brad Miller's *l*."

"Lucy." Dr. Bertel looked serious. "I understand what you are trying to say, honey, but I don't think we can know by the way Brad Miller writes his *l*s that he's going to become a big-time mobster. You know, writing changes as you grow up. I'm sure Brad's *l*s won't look like spears when he gets a bit older."

"Mom, do you look at your patients' writing before treating them?"

"No, I don't. Of course, many of my patients are just learning to write."

"Well, you should," said Lucy. "It might help you treat them."

"Funny. We didn't learn that in medical school," said Dr. Bertel.

"You probably had too many assemblies in medical school and there wasn't enough time left. Is there anything for dessert?" asked Lucy.

"Oh, no!" Dr. Bertel jumped up. "My pie! I forgot to put it in the oven. I can't believe it. How did this happen again? Oh, dear me. I'm afraid we have uncooked pie for dessert tonight."

Lucy and her dad looked at each other and laughed. Lucy's mom was known as one of the best pediatric surgeons in the country, and one of the worst bakers in Savannah. A lot had changed since they'd moved, but not that.

8:14 p.m.

Lucy and her father played Mancala after dinner. Then her mother made her take a shampoo-shower. Lucy didn't get back to her bedroom until 8:14 p.m., a full hour and thirty-six minutes after she'd left it. At eight thirty she was supposed to get into bed and read for half an hour. That gave her only sixteen minutes to focus on the note Pigeon had given her. Knowing there wasn't a whole lot she could find out in sixteen minutes, she started at the bottom.

Lucy felt relieved to see the windowsill empty. Pigeon would take time away from the note, time she didn't have to waste. She pulled a magnifying glass out of her desk drawer and placed it over the word "*Zelda.*" The first thing she noticed was the Z. Zelda's Z had something peculiar in it. Lucy couldn't quite figure it out. At first glance it looked almost magical, like a fairy had written it, but when she looked more closely, she could see tiny aberrations in the line. She knew Zelda was Nicky's grandmother, so perhaps her hands shook a little. Maybe that was all it was. Elderly people often got the shakes. People with annoying grandsons probably got pretty shaky too.

Lucy always started her handwriting analysis with the signature. Signatures were like fingerprints, all of them unique. You can tell a lot about someone from the way they sign their name—much more than most people realized.

LWR #5: EVERY SIGNATURE HAS A SECRET.

Lucy believed this as much as she believed the sun was hot. She couldn't prove it quite yet, but she was convinced that hidden deep inside every signature was a secret. Take Alice Walters, her babysitter back in Savannah. Alice acted cheerful all the time. She laughed at everything, even Lucy's fathers' jokes. She put a happy face instead of a regular dot over the *i* in "Alice," but if you looked at the way she crossed the *t* in "Walters," you could tell she was hiding an angry streak. Her *t* bar cut through the *l* on the left of the *t*, like she was trying to chop it in half, and on the right side it kept going all the way past the rest of the letters after it, like it was racing to get off the page. Does that sound like someone who is always happy?

Alice Walters

LWR #6: Cross people will cross more than their Ts.

Thump.
Thump, thump, thump.
Lucy looked up from the "Zelda" and did a

quick check for cracks in her ceiling. It was amazing that it hadn't fallen yet. Not that she could see any cracks, but with the constant pounding going on, it had to work harder at staying up than most ceilings, and someday, Lucy figured, it would simply crumble down on top of her.

Wherever he went earlier, I wish he'd go back there permanently, thought Lucy.

Thump.

Thump.

Thump.

The "elda" in "Zelda" had been written in one stroke, like pen and paper had been ballroom dance partners. *People don't write like this anymore,* thought Lucy. *People write in rap, not ballroom, these days.*

Lucy turned the note sideways so the words lined up like blades of grass. She rotated it again until it was upside down and looked at the letters not as letters, but as shapes. She held it up in the air above her head and examined it from underneath. Then she put it down on her desk and picked up a toothpick. She let the toothpick follow the flow of the letters, sliding down what people in the handwriting business called the descenders—into their

dips at the bottom of *y*s and *g*s—and climbing up
the ascenders—to the tops of the *t*s, *k*s, *d*s.

My Dearest Nicky,

*I must ask you to sneak out and come see
your grandma Zelda. A matter of the utmost
urgency has come to my attention.*

Thump. Bang. Boom.

Does he ever stop jumping around? wondered
Lucy. *How's a person supposed to concentrate?*

Lucy took a deep breath and continued tracing.

*We'll have pie. Remember always, from dawn
to dusk, in cold weather and warm, that your
grandma Zelda loves you. Come soon as a
raccoon.*

Your grandma,

Zelda

Thump.

Thump, thump, thump, thump, thump, thump, thump, thump.

Bang. Thump.

Lucy looked at the clock. 8:24. She had six minutes left. That boy Nicky didn't deserve to get a
note with this kind of handwriting. Maybe she'd
keep it for just a week or two. Lucy thought about
quickly Skyping the Wrighties to see what they
thought she should do. She hadn't talked to them
in ages, but she could sure use them now. She
looked at the clock again. 8:25. Not enough time
left to Skype before incoming parents. She should
probably give Nicky the note soon. She knew that.
It looked important. But honestly, the kind of
note that someone who spent his life jumping on
the floor deserved was from scary Brad Miller. An
original handwriting sample like this would be a
great addition to her collection. Maybe it was more
important for her to study the letters than for Nicky
to get the note. Lucy thought this would be a good
ethical question tomorrow night at dinner. *If you
receive an urgent note intended for somebody who isn't
worthy of it, should you give it to him anyway?*

Thump.

Thump.

Th-th-thump.

No, she thought. *I'm not giving away handwriting like this to anyone who makes that much noise.* Lucy got up from her desk and ran down the hallway. She grabbed a mop from the broom closet and grasped the pole with both hands. She returned to her room determined to have a little chat with the headache-inducing stomper, in his own language. She heaved the end of the pole up against her ceiling.

Bam. Bam.

She pounded again to make sure he got the message. It never hurts to double check things.

Thump.

Thump.

Thump.

Bam. Bam. Bam. Bam.

Bam. Bam.

Silence.

Lucy looked at the clock. 8:27. Only three minutes left. She sat down at the desk and picked up the note.

Thump.

Thump.

Badunk.

That did it. Lucy grabbed a pen and a piece of paper from her drawer and wrote her own note in her meanest Genghis Khan handwriting.

NICKY,

THIS IS A CEASE-AND-DESIST ORDER!

STOP MAKING SO MUCH NOISE UP THERE!

YOUR UNDERHEAD NEIGHBOR,

LUCY

"Mom, I'll be back in two minutes. I promise," she called out before the front door slammed behind her.

PART FOUR

THURSDAY, APRIL 1
7:55 a.m.
West 68th Street, Apartment 7D

"But I want to walk my favorite brother to school," said Stella.

Nicky turned around to see if there was another brother hiding behind him. Being the only brother didn't necessarily give you favorite-brother status. It barely gave you human status. Technically three people lived in the Gibsons' apartment, but Nicky often felt like he lived alone. He was hardly a brother, much less a favorite brother.

"Why?" asked Nicky.

"I told you," said Stella. "You're my favorite brother, and I want to make sure you get to school safely."

"Is this an April Fools' Day trick?" he asked. On April Fools' Day Nicky prepared himself for the worst. He double-knotted his laces, watched what he ate, never walked under a ladder, and stayed away from the number thirteen. On April Fools' Day he didn't leave the house without a bag filled with provisions that included a map, a flashlight, a can of soda, trail mix, creamy peanut butter, bread, and his wallet that had twenty-two dollars in it. You'd think April Fools' Day would be one of Nicky's favorite days. A boy like him could probably plan some memorable pranks. Instead it was like the anti-Christmas. Terrible things happened to Nicky on April Fools' Day. His cat died on April Fools' Day. (She wasn't just sleeping, like he thought.) He broke his leg on April Fools' Day. (It wasn't just nothing, like he thought.) And his mom moved to India on April Fools' Day. (She wasn't just taking a vacation, like he thought.) Nicky knew enough to prepare himself for anything, even an earthquake, even Stella wanting to take him to school.

"This isn't an April Fools' Day trick. I don't do those," said Stella. "Can't a sister want to take her brother to school on April first without it being a trick?"

"I don't know. The sister didn't want to take the brother to school on any other day," said Nicky suspiciously.

"That's not true," said Stella.

"Name one."

Stella thought about it. "The first day of school, but you wouldn't let me. I've wanted to take you every day since then. I love taking you to school. You really should let me do it more often."

Nicky squinted his eyes and stared at Stella with all his might. He tried to see through her skin, or into her eyes, or up her nose, or past her braces and into her mouth, to get a glimpse of her brain so he could figure out what was really going on. Stella's hair had returned to curly and brown, but she still wore thick dark lines under her eyes. Her lips were bright orange today. She had applied a layer of pinkish skin color over her already pinkish skin, to make a second skin, which was impossible to see through. He couldn't get past the lines on her eyes, either, and when he got up close to look up her nose, she yelled, "Stop that! Now!"

Nicky's school was five blocks from their house. Stella's school was six blocks away. They shared the same first two blocks, but then Nicky turned right and Stella kept walking straight. If this wasn't an April Fools' Day trick, something important must be on one of his extra three blocks. He mentally walked down each of the blocks. The first one had nothing but apartment buildings on it, not even doorman buildings. The second and third blocks had a mix of apartment buildings and stores. Stella probably wanted something in one of those stores. She would do almost anything to go shopping, even if it meant being nice to her brother.

"Sure, you can walk me to school," said Nicky, mostly because he wanted to know why she was paying attention to him.

"Bye, Dad," Nicky yelled out.

"Why do you bother?" Stella asked.

"I don't know," said Nicky. "Maybe he likes it when I say good-bye."

"Maybe," said Stella. "I don't really think he cares, though. Come on. I don't want you to be late."

Nicky gave Stella the who-are-you-and-where'd-you-put-my-sister look. It's a look he had never had an opportunity to use before, so he hadn't perfected it.

"Stop giving me that sick hippo face and move! Now!" she shouted.

The real Stella had returned. She checked herself in the mirror by the front door and pushed her hair back behind her shoulders, then swung the door open and rushed out.

On his way out Nicky noticed a piece of paper with his name on it taped to the front door. *Not a good sign,* he thought. He grabbed it and quickly stuffed it into his pocket. He'd read it later, maybe tomorrow after April Fools' Day had safely passed, as if that were possible. For now he'd focus on getting to school without anything terrible happening.

Stella pressed on the arrow button until the tip of her finger turned red. "If you've made us late, I'm never going to forgive you," she snapped.

"You don't have to walk me to school," Nicky said.

The elevator door opened, and they stepped inside. Stella tapped her right foot on the floor and stood with her nose flush to the door for the entire ride down. When they reached the lobby, she grabbed Nicky by his shirt and blew out of the building.

A block later Nicky learned the real reason for the new sister love, and like she'd said, it had nothing to do with an April Fools' Day trick. The reason's name was Max. Max lived on Sixty-ninth Street, one block from them, and walked his little sister to school every day. Turned out Max's sister went to Nicky's school. Turned out that Stella just loved walking her little brother to school too. "How cool is that? We can walk them to school together."

"Yeah, I guess," said Max.

Nicky looked over at his sister. Turned out she did know how to smile.

So far things seemed to be working out. Perhaps Nicky's day wouldn't be so bad after all, or perhaps it was about to get a whole lot worse.

8:30 a.m.
Apartment 8G

At eight thirty, Nicky gave an incorrect answer in math class. (21 was the correct answer. Nicky'd calculated 10. The question: Find the area of a rectangle when l=7 and w=3.) At the same time, his father opened the door to Grandma Zelda's apartment for two people, both standing straight and stiff in form-fitted jackets. Nicky answered a second question wrong while Mr. Gibson showed the people around the apartment. Nicky was telling his teacher he'd have gotten the third answer right but he had to go to the bathroom really badly and couldn't concentrate (his teacher suggested he start to concentrate or else he'd be using the bathroom in the principal's office) while Mr. Gibson led the people into Grandma Zelda's kitchen. One of the them, the woman, shuddered and yipped after seeing a pigeon on the windowsill.

Pigeon had been patiently waiting for some Zeldaberry pie for breakfast and hadn't expected to be insulted first thing in the morning. She lifted her wings unnaturally high—she actually cramped up on her right side—and pushed them down in a big slow-motion, glorious germ-spreading flap.

The woman shrieked and threw her hand up against her mouth. Pigeon plumped herself up and made some mental notes. The man had a striped tie dangling down his shirt, and the woman's hair was pushed up, off her face, into a puffy nesting hairdo. (According to a survey Pigeon once conducted, seven out of ten people that wore their hair in an up-nesting-do crossed the street when they saw a bird.)

"The paperwork is taken care of. Let's sit down and I'll show it to you," said Mr. Gibson, who looked like his usual gray-shirted, gray-panted self. Pigeon realized for the first time that Mr. Gibson sounded gray too, kind of like a thunderous gray day.

He handed tie-man a folder. "Here's the deed. You see, it's signed and dated."

What's a deed? wondered Pigeon.

"Ahem."

Pigeon was so startled by Mr. Gibson's throat roar that she practically toppled backward off the windowsill.

"I think we should set the asking price at fifty thousand dollars," said the woman with the nest on her head. She smiled. Her two front top teeth were also wearing glossy red lipstick.

"Not enough. Not nearly enough," replied Mr. Gibson. His hand slammed down onto the table. The man and the woman abruptly pushed their chairs away from the table and Mr. Gibson's sonic boom of a voice.

Nest-hairdo spoke softly, as if to encourage Mr. Gibson to speak more quietly through example. "Naturally I never want to be negative. You need time to think. Were you planning to paint? Did you care to clean? And what's that scent? Blueberry? Raspberry? Huckleberry? Apartments with surprising or strange smells scarcely sell."

"YOU HAVE TO CONSIDER WHAT A DOWN MARKET CAN HANDLE," shouted tie-man. Pigeon figured his approach was to try to match Mr. Gibson's decibel.

"April Fools'! Right? Ha, ha," Mr. Gibson fake-laughed.

"No jokes. We're offering our official opinion," said nest-hairdo. Mr. Gibson dropped his head into his hands. The tie-man played with his earlobe, and nest hairdo checked her watch. "Fine," said Mr. Gibson. "Fifty thousand. But sell the apartment immediately."

Pigeon felt her feathers ruffle. Her bill began to shake and her crown rose up toward the sky in a vicious triangle as she began to make sense of what was happening.

Nest-hairdo stood up first. "Wonderful. We'll get to work."

Tie-man stuck his hand out toward Mr. Gibson. "We'll be in touch."

Mr. Gibson followed the pair out of the kitchen. Pigeon heard the voices peter out, then the slam of a door. She listened, but all she heard now was the echo of emptiness. She looked into the kitchen and thought about crashing through the invisible wall to find out where Grandma Zelda had been hiding during all this, but she restrained herself. Rules are made for a reason.

12:15 p.m.
Apartment 6D

Lately Lucy had been scoring in the 65 to 75 percent range on her signature tests. A lucky amateur could do that. Sure, sometimes she'd get 100 percent, but just as often she'd rate dismally, in the 20 to 30 percent range. One miserable afternoon she scored a measly 5 percent. That's when Lucy decided to become a master forger. If she knew how to make a fake, she'd know how to spot a fake. She could see what kind of ink splotches a pen made when someone stopped to think midletter and what happened to that letter when they started writing again.

Sitting at her desk, hunched over a piece of parchment paper, her hand trembled. She was pushing down too hard, and her John Hancock had wiggles and bubbles and three ink splotches. John Hancock had the best John Hancock, even if other people's John Hancocks looked like John Hancock's John Hancock. Lucy's John Hancock didn't remotely resemble Hancock's John Hancock. She had a long way to go, like to the top of Mount Everest and back, before even her *J* came close.

Lucy knew, by looking at the elaborate flourishes and loopy letters, that that John Hancock had probably spent years practicing his signature, and she imagined the conversation the founding fathers must have had.

John Hancock: I've been working on my signature since I was a lad of four.

Benjamin Franklin: Thomas, my friend, you must see my magnificent signature before you choose who should be the first to sign the Declaration of Independence.

Hancock: My signature will be so large that King George will not need his spectacles to view it.

Franklin: Yes, but as the eldest of the signers, I believe it is self-evident that I should be the first to sign.

Hancock: With all due respect, Ben, your hand is showing its age. Your line is no longer smooth.

Thomas Jefferson: This is a difficult decision. Ben, I'm sorry, old chap, but John's signature is as beautiful as my words. He'll be the first to sign the Declaration of Independence.

(Lucy wondered if Thomas Jefferson would have been upset that people talked more about John Hancock's signature than about the rest of the Declaration of Independence. It was his own fault for asking John Hancock to sign, knowing he had the kind of signature that people were probably going to talk about.)

Lucy's quill pen lurched across the paper. Her John was a failure; her Hancock looked more like "Hancook" or even "handshake" than Hancock.

LWR #7: If it's your name, you do the best at writing it the same.

She looked up at her window and saw Pigeon. "Oh, hi," she said.

"Why are you home? Are you sick? Did you get in trouble?" asked Pigeon.

Lucy answered Pigeon's questions in reverse order.

"No, no, and today's a half day."

Pigeon checked the sky. The sun sat smack in the middle of it. "Half day" didn't make sense. If anything, today would be a longer than usual day. "No, today is a full day," said Pigeon.

"No, it's not," said Lucy. "First they called us down to the auditorium and told us we were having a surprise test. Then they said 'April Fools'.' Then they sent us back to our classrooms and double April-Foolsed us by telling us there was no test and it was a half day. So you see, it's a half day."

"That's a lot to keep track of," said Pigeon, sighing. "I still think today will have two halves, though."

Lucy figured out why Pigeon was confused, and smiled. She started writing again. Up, across, and down. Loop back up to the diagonal. Pick up pen, circle down, and—"Look at this! I jiggled on the *h*. My *h* looks like a snake with warts."

"That's too bad," said Pigeon. "Remember the note from yesterday? Will you read it to me now?" asked Pigeon. "There's something terribly odd going on."

Lucy put the quill pen into a jar of water and opened a folder. "I started a Zelda file. I'm planning on working with this note after I get one okay-looking John Hancock. Pigeon, it's practically impossible to find old-fashioned handwriting these days. The ink on this note is still fresh. I can't even believe how lucky I am to have this. You can tell that Zelda is old from the little wrinkles in her letters. They look like tiny wiggles; you can barely detect them."

LWR #8: OLD PEOPLE GET WRINKLES, IN THEIR WRITING TOO.

Pigeon sighed and said, "Please start reading. It's kind of an emergency."

"Is it an emergency or kind of an emergency?" asked Lucy. "Wait, never mind. Don't answer that. That's the type of question my father would ask. No one should ever have to answer those kinds of questions."

Lucy smiled and started to read.

My Dearest Nicky,

I must ask you to sneak out and come see your grandma Zelda. A matter of the utmost

urgency has come to my attention. We'll have
pie. Remember always, from dawn to dusk, in
cold weather and warm, that your grandma
Zelda loves you. Come soon as a raccoon.

Your grandma,

Zelda

"What do you think?" asked Lucy.

"Oh, dear," said Pigeon. "We need to get this to
Nicky right away."

Pigeon looked up at the sun. Soon it would start
its journey across the city. Once it started to move,
Nicky would be leaving school. Pigeon looked up at
the sun again. It hadn't moved yet. *Maybe it's stuck,*
thought Pigeon. *Maybe I should fly up there and give
it a push.*

2:45 p.m.
Around the West Side

Pigeon waited for Nicky in a tree near his school. Pigeon watched two girls kick a backpack like it was a soccer ball, and a boy with blond curly hair buy a pretzel from a street vendor. Pigeon saw no signs of Nicky.

She flew back to his apartment building on Sixty-eighth Street, traveling the route that Nicky should have taken and would have taken, were he a child other than Nicky. Pigeon stopped to collect her thoughts on a branch of a ginkgo tree on Sixty-ninth Street but found herself unable to collect anything because the tree was loaded with sparrows that had found a dark green car parked below to use for target practice.

"Good one!"

"Nice!"

"I got the window!"

"Splat! Mine went splat!"

"Move over. My turn!"

Wow, thought Pigeon. *You'd think sparrows would have something better to do with their time.* She abandoned the tree and headed for an empty streetlight to devise a flight plan. Trying to think like Nicky never did any good because he didn't have a particular way of thinking. You'd think he'd head toward the park—which means he probably didn't, so you'd start thinking that he didn't, which means he probably did.

Pigeon flew in the direction no typical boy would walk and spotted Nicky twelve blocks from his school, seventeen blocks away from his building. He was heading in the direction of nothing interesting for a boy his age. He flapped his arms and jumped but never got more than eight inches off the ground. He was headed into midtown, a place filled with wealthy business people, who rarely fed pigeons, and homeless people, who often shared their food. (That was one of the many things about the city that Pigeon never could understand. She knew it to be a fact. She had conducted a survey.) Against her better judgment Pigeon landed on the sidewalk directly in front of Nicky's left foot.

"Nicky," she whisper-shouted as his foot swung in the direction of her head. "Watch out!"

Nicky's face widened; his eyes brightened; his mouth opened and his foot stopped in the air. "Hi, Pigeon. What are you do—" He glanced down the street to make sure no one would see him talking to a pigeon, and finished his sentence, "Why are you here?"

"I need to tell you something important. Why are you in this neighborhood?" asked Pigeon.

Nicky shrugged his shoulders and looked up at a street sign. "Oh, no," he yelped and took off running at top speed. He tore around corners, zig-zagged through people, jumped over fire hydrants, tripped over a leash that stretched across the side-walk, and tumbled onto a woman wearing a red dress. In spite of all this, he got home in record-setting time and disappeared through the front door of his apartment building.

"Didn't you hear me when I said I needed to tell you something important?" huffed Pigeon. She had followed Nicky back to Sixty-eighth Street and perched herself outside his bedroom window.

"I don't remember," said Nicky.

"Are you sure you don't remember?" asked Pigeon.

"Almost-positive sure," replied Nicky.

"Well, I am positive sure that I told you I had something important to tell you and you ran away from me."

"I didn't want to get home from school late."

"Then perhaps you shouldn't have walked in the wrong direction," suggested Pigeon. "Now, can you stand right there and watch the clouds while I get something for you? Will you remember to stay there and not move? No matter what, don't leave your room."

"I have to stay in my room. I'm in time-out."

"Good," said Pigeon. "Remember, don't move." She hopped over to the edge of his windowsill, then stopped herself. "How about if I just tell you what was written on your grandmother's note? You don't like to read anyway."

"You got the note? What'd it say? Where is it?" Nicky asked.

"It's in a safe place. Don't worry." Pigeon glanced at the sky and whistled. "In very nice handwriting your grandmother suggested that you sneak out immediately and visit her because a raccoon is coming. I can tell you for a fact that there's something as unpleasant as a sparrows' convention going on upstairs. I'd recommend that you do what your grandmother says and go to her right away."

"I can't."

"Why not?"

"I told you. I'm in time-out. I'm always in time-out. I can't do anything without getting in trouble, not even be two minutes late from school."

"You were more than two minutes late." Pigeon believed it was her duty to remind Nicky of the facts.

"I told my father I was late for an April Fools' trick. I wanted him to think I was running away."

"What did he say to that?" asked Pigeon.

"He said he understood, and not to worry about anything," said Nicky.

"That's good, isn't it?"

"Then he said, 'April Fools' and sent me to my room."

"Oh," said Pigeon. "Not so good after all. Well, at least maybe your father's getting a sense of humor."

"Maybe," said Nicky. Maybe his dad wasn't a secret superhero but was a secret comedian. That would be king. Everybody thought he was mean, so nobody suspected he was the funniest guy in the world. He got so funny that people literally started dying of laughter, so he had to stop being funny, and he became mean. But sometimes, secretly, he was still funny. Nicky sighed. Chances were, his father wasn't really a secret comedian.

"It's not fair. I didn't do anything wrong. I never do anything wrong."

"Well, actually," said Pigeon, "there was that time you ended up on the highway and the police had to close it down to come rescue you."

"That was one time," said Nicky.

"Well, actually, do you remember the time— Oh, never mind," said Pigeon.

"I'm going to see Grandma Zelda. She told me to sneak out. So that's what I'm going to do. Just like in the movies. You know how people know how to sneak into places and out of places really well in the movies?"

Pigeon thought about some of the movies she had seen (she watched a lot of them on big-screen

TVs from windowsills) and didn't much like the fact that usually when there was a bird in a movie it meant something bad was going to happen. Or it meant somebody was about to fall in love. As if all birds stood for was love and doom.

"My dad will never even know I'm gone. Do you want to come?"

Pigeon looked back at the tip of her wing, hoping it would make the decision for her.

3:24 p.m.
Apartment 7D
Movie Script

<u>FADE IN</u>

NICKY OPENS HIS DOOR AND LOOKS OUT INTO THE HALLWAY.

NICKY

(whispers)

Hello?

Is anyone out here?

HE TIPTOES OUT OF HIS ROOM. THE FLOORBOARDS CREAK AND NICKY JUMPS

UP. HE STEPS MORE CAREFULLY. AFTER SIX
STEPS WE HEAR A THUNDEROUSLY LOUD
CREAK.

NICKY

Did anyone hear that?

NICKY WAITS IN SILENCE FOR A MOMENT,
THEN RESUMES WALKING UNTIL A HAND
GRABS HIM FROM BEHIND.

NICKY

Arghh! What are you doing here?

STELLA

What are *you* doing here? Aren't you in time-
out again? Go back to your room, or I'm going
to tell Dad you're stealing money from him.

NICKY

That's not true, though.

STELLA

I know. But it's April Fools' Day.

NICKY

You said you didn't do April Fools' Day tricks.
If you tell Dad that I stole money, I won't tell
you about the urgent top-secret note from
Grandma Zelda.

STELLA

Yeah, right, secret note. Good one. April Fools'.
Hardy-har.

STELLA WALKS OFF DOWN THE HALLWAY,
SHAKING HER HEAD. NICKY WAITS UNTIL
SHE'S IN HER ROOM, THEN RUSHES TO THE
FRONT DOOR.
HE CAREFULLY OPENS THE DOOR, BUT IT
MAKES A FIRECRACKER-LOUD SOUND.

NICKY'S FATHER (HEARD OFF CAMERA)

Yes, I am glad you already found someone
interested in the apartment. I will see you
upstairs tomorrow at six o'clock.

NICKY LEAVES THE APARTMENT.

FADE OUT

We now return to our regularly scheduled paragraphs.

3:30 p.m.
Apartment 8G

Grandma Zelda didn't answer her doorbell the first time Nicky rang. The second time, he pressed down on the buzzer and counted to a hundred, although he knew that if Grandma Zelda didn't have her ears in, he could count to a million and she still wouldn't hear him.

Her note had instructed him to sneak out. She'd be expecting him. Nicky turned the doorknob and heard a gulping sound but wasn't sure if it came from him or the door. He pushed. The door swung open, but the doorknob remained behind, in Nicky's hand. "Oh, no," he whispered to himself. "I hope I don't get in trouble for this."

Nicky called out for her. "Grandma Zelda?

"Grandma?" he called out again after he didn't get a response. "Grandma. Grandma Zelda?"

He walked into the kitchen. He looked at the window and waved to Pigeon. He checked for Grandma Zelda in the bedroom. He saw her viola d'amore resting on the bed, alone. Nicky looked around the sides of her bed, in case she had fallen off it. He looked under the bed, in case she'd rolled under it. He looked for her in the bathroom, the shower, and the cabinets.

"Grandma?"

He pushed his way into her two closets, behind her housecoats and dresses.

"Grandma? Grandma Zelda?"

Back in the hallway.

"Grandma Zelda, is this an April Fools' Day trick?"

"Grandma Zelda?" he called out again. He looked around until he determined that his grandmother was missing. Now, many things commonly go missing during the course of a typical day. These tend to include keys, shoes, pens, and homework. Grandmothers tend not to be on the list. Grandmothers are a rather reliable type. At least this was certainly the case with Grandma Zelda. She baked. She listened to music and played viola d'amore; she told lots of stories; she stayed at home. Only, this was April Fools' Day, and Nicky knew that unless Grandma Zelda was playing her own April

Fools' Day trick, something terrible had happened to her. Since he doubted that his grandmother even knew it was April Fools' Day—she had a hard time remembering what year it was, never mind what day it was—Nicky had a stomach-churning feeling that his life was about to change for the worse again.

He ambled out of Grandma Zelda's apartment. "Okay," he said to the doorknob in his hand. "Do you know where Grandma Zelda is?"

Nicky leaned his back up against the wall and slid down to the floor in front of the elevator. He carefully examined the doorknob, like it was some ancient artifact that he had just excavated, until something white caught his eye. Nicky rolled the doorknob down the long narrow hallway. He reached across the floor and picked up a piece of paper.

Help me.

Zelda Gibson

"Stella, I'm not kidding," said Nicky.

"I'm not going to fall for some April Fools' Day trick. Not now, not ever." Stella stood in front of the mirror and stuck out her tongue.

"Bhat bo you sink of bierced pongues?" she asked.

"What?" Nicky shook his head and scowled.

Stella slipped her tongue back into her mouth. "What do you think of pierced tongues?"

"I think they're disgusting," said Nicky. "And if you do pierce yours, I'm going to tell Dad. Can we talk about this later? I need to show you something important."

"Well, I'm not going to do it, but not because you'd tell Dad. Anyway, I know you wouldn't. You're too scared of him. I'm not doing it because I think it's disgusting too. Wow, what do you know? There is something we agree on."

"Stella, I'm not kidding. Grandma Zelda's gone. I found a note that she wrote and it says 'Help me' on it, and now she's missing. We've got to do something. Look." Nicky held out the piece of paper with the words "Help me. Zelda Gibson" written on it for Stella to see.

"Yeah, right. I'll believe that Grandma Zelda is missing and you happened to find this note if you'll believe that Justin Bieber is my boyfriend."

"But I'm not kidding."

"So, have you told Dad, then? Don't you think he should know? Grandma Zelda is his mother, after all."

"I think you should tell him. He'll believe it if you tell him, and I'll get sent to my room and yelled at for lying if I tell him—even though I'm not lying. I swear I'm not. And I have proof. I have the note."

"Nice try. I'm not falling for some April Fools' trick. There's no way in this world that I'd set myself up for a time-out by telling Dad some silly story about Grandma Zelda going missing and a 'Help me' note. Do you think I'm that dumb? I don't think Dad much likes April Fools' Day, and I don't think you're very funny with this whole Grandma Zelda missing story. Ugh, my room is starting to smell bad, and it's not because of me. I think you've been in here for way too long. Aren't you supposed to be in a time-out anyway? Dad!" Stella called out.

"You're mean," said Nicky. He slammed Stella's door and stomped across the hallway into his room. He looked out his window. Where was Pigeon? Why didn't she come back?

9:30 p.m.
Apartment 6D

"But you got an A+. Why are you so upset?" Mr. Bertel said to Lucy.

"Dad, can't you see it?" Lucy replied. Her voice cracked. "The first time I wasn't positive, but this time I'm sure. Look at Mrs. Costa's writing on my last two papers. Now compare them with her writing on my papers from last semester."

Mr. Bertel reread the comment on Lucy's paper. *Great research! Excellent evidence to support your thesis.* He smiled, as any father would.

"The letters look beyond miserably sad," said Lucy. "I think Mrs. Costa's life is falling apart, or worse. She's probably getting fired. She's could be sick and getting divorced and kicked out of her apartment, too. Dad, some of her letters are so light you can barely see them. It's like she isn't strong enough to keep the pen on the paper. And then some of her letters are really dark, like the weight of the world was in her pen. There's got to be something you can do to help her."

"Lucy, Mrs. Costa is dandy. She's hunky-dory. Her life is superb. Really, there is nothing for you to worry about." Mr. Bertel never used the word "great" anymore. He knew Lucy had given up on the word "great," so he tended to replace "great" with all sorts of other rather silly words.

"Dad, can't you see it? The older writing is full and round and loopy. Now look at this." Lucy picked up a piece of paper. "It looks like someone let all the air out of the letters. Look at her *a*, it's almost an undotted *i*. Are you telling me that's not a problem?"

"Honestly, Lucy, that's what I'm saying. Mrs. Costa is feeling snazzy," Mr. Bertel placed his hand on Lucy's head.

"Dad, that's like looking at a big black cloud and saying you don't think it's going to rain. Don't you believe the handwriting is telling the truth?" Lucy's voice quivered.

"I believe that you believe it. I can't say I'm a believer, though."

"Dad, you have to believe."

"A healthy dose of skepticism isn't a bad thing. You know I'm a mathematician. We like our theorems proven. Show me proof about letters suddenly deflating and I'll become a believer. I insist on proof." Mr. Bertel looked over at the purple numbers on the clock next to Lucy's bed. "For instance, I have proof that it is past your bedtime, which means you should be asleep and not worrying about Mrs. Costa."

"Dad, I have proof. Look. Right here." She pulled her handwriting analysis journal out from under her pillow and handed it to her father.

LWR #9: LIFE CHANGES LEAD TO LETTER CHANGES.

Mr. Bertel shook his head. "Sorry. I need concrete evidence about Mrs. Costa, not speculative science. Lucy, you need to go to sleep immediately."

"It's not speculative science," said Lucy. "You can really learn about people through their handwriting."

"Sleep," insisted Mr. Bertel.

"I'm serious, Dad," said Lucy.

"Me too," responded Mr. Bertel. "Sleep. Now. I love you." And with that he kissed the top of her head and turned off the light.

Lucy listened to her father's footsteps as they made their way down the long hallway to her parents' bedroom, and she made a mental list of all that had happened in the past few days.

> Got April-Foolsed and let out of school early.
>
> Got new handwriting sample, but felt a little guilty about not giving it to jumping-boy Nicky.
>
> Wrote a John Hancock that looked not altogether terrible.
>
> Discovered teacher was having a major life crisis.

When she could no longer hear any floorboards creaking, she jumped out of bed and ran to her window. "Pigeon," she called out, "where are you?"

Great Research!

Excellent evidence to support your thesis.

11:40 p.m.
Apartment 7D

The moon looked too large, almost like the real moon had been replaced by a rounder, brighter pretend April Fools' moon. Sleep didn't come for Nicky. His mind wouldn't get off its treadmill. Nicky emptied the books out of his backpack and hid them under his bed. He stuffed a shirt, pair of pants, underwear, socks, and toothbrush into his backpack and double-checked to make sure all his April Fools' Day provisions were still there. He thought about writing a note for his dad, but he didn't much like writing so decided not to. Then he returned to bed and closed his eyes, but his brain took off with more thoughts. It kept moving, faster, faster, faster in every direction but one.

Pigeon stared up at the moon instead of sleeping. Every time she shifted positions and tried to escape from the glow, the big orange moon showed up and snatched her dreams right out of her head. Pigeon stood there staring at the big bully of a moon, wondering if it was enjoying the dreams that were supposed to be hers. She turned her head from it and flew across the park toward Nicky's window. She was sure he'd already be asleep but decided to check on him.

"What are you doing here? I needed you earlier," whispered Nicky. He looked at his clock. He checked to make sure his door was closed.

"Couldn't sleep. Too much moon. What are you doing awake?" said Pigeon.

"Moon problems too." Nicky looked out his window at the giant moon and added, "And that's the smallest of my problems." He jumped off his bed and showed Pigeon the "Help me" note. For the next twelve minutes they whispered back and forth and devised a plan. Tomorrow they would search the entire city if they needed to. Tomorrow they would find Grandma Zelda.

One window down Lucy slept, although fitfully. Her sheer orange and yellow curtains didn't do much to prevent the big moon from entering her room, nor did they convince the shadows on her walls to stop making letters. An hour after her father had kissed her good night, Lucy had called him back in to tell him she couldn't sleep. He'd told her to keep trying. Lucy closed her eyes for as long as she could keep them closed without sleeping. When she opened them, she saw a shadow splashed across her wall that looked like Eleanor Roosevelt's signature. Even in shadow, the *R* in "Roosevelt" loomed larger than the *E* in "Eleanor." Lucy figured the large *R* meant she must have been proud to be President Roosevelt's wife.

Before midnight Lucy heard some thumping on her ceiling. She tried to fall asleep again but couldn't for the longest time. Sometimes no matter how hard you try, falling asleep is one of the hardest things to do.

Eleanor Roosevelt

PART FIVE

Nicky left early for school. He didn't actually plan on going to school, which is why he was running early. There's nothing that better motivates a boy to wake up and get to school early than knowing he's not planning on going. On a normal day Nicky dragged his backpack into the elevator at 8:05 in the morning. Today he flung his backpack over his right shoulder and stepped into the elevator at precisely 7:40 a.m.

At 7:40 and thirty-four seconds the elevator stopped on the sixth floor and Lucy walked in. Her black hair and light brown skin, along with those big eyes, made Nicky think of Jasmine from the movie *Aladdin*. Lucy tilted her head to the side, as if her right ear weighed too much. Her mouth opened, and a greeting popped out.

"Hi. I'm Lucy."

She surprised herself by saying anything; she just hadn't had enough day in her day yet to reconsider talking to her head-stomper. (As usual her dad had woke her up at six o'clock in the morning to say he was leaving, Mom would make breakfast, and he'd see Lucy-loo at school-ioo. This happened every day. She couldn't figure out why her dad felt compelled to wake her up each morning to say the same thing he'd said the morning before and the one before that. She'd either fall back asleep and oversleep or not be able to fall back asleep and feel too tired to think all day at school. Mornings were brutal. Someone should outlaw them.)

Since she'd already broken ground and started talking to Nicky, she decided to keep digging.

"I taped a note to your front door the other morning. Did you get it?"

"You did that?" Nicky replied.

"Did you get it?" Lucy repeated her question.

They passed by the fourth floor.

"Yeah. Thanks."

"Did you read it?" After enduring months of miserable head banging, Lucy felt like putting him on the spot. She stomped her foot three times on the elevator floor to help jog his memory in case it was clogged up. She searched for his eyes under his floppy hair to see if they looked shifty. If he had shifty eyes, like she suspected, he'd lie and pretend he didn't get her note.

"Um, I didn't have time to, but I think I still have it."

Nicky pushed his hand deep into his pocket and pulled out a crumpled piece of paper. "Hold this," he said, and handed Lucy the "Help me" note. He couldn't imagine what was so important that the girl from 6D had to give him a hand-delivered note. He hastily started to unfold it, which resulted in his ripping it in half. "Oops," he said, and fumbled to realign the two torn pieces.

Second floor.

"What's this?" asked Lucy. She held up the "Help me" note.

"My grandma Zelda wrote it."

Lobby.

The elevator door opened, but neither of them stepped out. The door closed and the elevator went up.

"Where'd you get it?" gulped Lucy.

"I found it near the elevator on the eighth floor. My grandmother lives in apartment 8G. I went to visit her, but she wasn't home. When I was leaving,

I found that note. Something bad must have happened to her, because she never leaves her apartment, and yesterday was April Fools' Day, and bad things always happen on April Fools' Day." He paused. "I'm cutting school to look for her."

"Who's seen this?" asked Lucy

"No one, really," said Nicky. "Well, one person. Actually, not a person. Never mind. Just so you know, I don't make noise."

Fifth floor.

"What do you mean? You jump around all afternoon, every afternoon."

"Jumping doesn't make noise," explained Nicky.

"When your ceiling is underneath the floor of the person jumping, it sounds like a thunderstorm that never passes."

"Oh, I didn't know that. That must be bad if you don't like thunder."

Seventh floor.

"Do you like thunder?" Nicky asked, hoping Lucy was one of those storm-chaser kind of girls who lived for the next big hurricane and hated sunny days.

"NO, I DON'T. I DETEST THUNDER!"

Ninth floor.

"What do you think happened to your grand-mother?" asked Lucy.

Until now Nicky had forced himself to not imagine any scenarios that could have led to Grandma Zelda writing a "Help me" note, because if he started to play a scenario out in his head, it involved something rotten or worse happening to her. Most people don't write "Help me" notes when they go on a vacation. They write them when something happens that involves blood, which is why Nicky forced himself to change his brain channel and think about other things.

Before Nicky got a chance to answer, the elevator door opened on the tenth floor, and a lady and a boy got in. "Good morning to you," said the lady, all singsongy. "How are you children today?"

"Fine," mumbled Nicky.

"Good," coughed Lucy.

On the way down the lady mentioned the weather—"Unseasonably warm—unreasonably warm, I might add"—the time of day—"The early birds are out"—and the flowers—"Looks like they've popped up before the showers." When the elevator reached the lobby, the chipper lady and quiet boy got out. Nicky and Lucy remained inside.

The door closed, but the elevator didn't move.

"Where are you going to look for her?" asked Lucy.

"I'm going to search the entire city, or the world if I need to, until I find her," said Nicky.

"Wow." Lucy gently rubbed her fingers over the words on the note to feel for bumps or inconsistencies. "Do you want help?" she asked. "I can help you." She realized she was offering to help the very boy who had been driving her crazy for seven months, but how could she resist a mystery like this one, one that came with handwritten notes? The elevator started going up again. "Meet me at the Society Library after school," she said.

(Lucy and her father had a tradition of going to the library on Friday afternoons. They'd done this when they'd lived in Savannah and had started their routine up again, without missing one Friday, after they'd moved. Now they generally went to the New York Society Library, partly because it was close to school and partly because of the book dungeon. You got there by taking a rickety old elevator with a creaky gate. To Lucy the books in the book dungeon looked, smelled, and felt more real than the books at the bookstore. She liked the biographies best. All winter long she'd sat at a metal desk in a dimly lit corner of the book dungeon and read about Benedict Arnold. He was two-timing during the Revolutionary War—spying for the British even though he was supposed to be on our side. She'd read everything she could find about him in the book dungeon. Then back at home she'd searched online for samples of his handwriting. Benedict Arnold should never have been trusted. If only someone had looked at the way he wrote his *d* in "Arnold." It flips back to the *A*. His letters weren't even loyal. A good *d* stays with itself.)

"I guess I can meet you at the Society Library," Nicky said.

He wasn't sure how he'd know when after school was, since he wasn't going to school, and he didn't know where the Society Library was, but he figured he'd have already found Grandma Zelda by then, so it didn't matter much.

They passed the third floor.

"I'll wait for you under the black canopy on

Seventy-ninth Street and Madison. Also, do you think I can keep this note for today?" She flashed the "Help me" note in front of his face. "I'll give it back to you this afternoon. Don't worry about it. It's in good hands."

Nicky looked at Lucy's hands. He was about to tell her that her hands looked good enough to him, and she could hold on to the note, when the elevator door opened on the twelfth floor. A man with a small fluffy dog walked in.

"I hope you kids weren't planning on going up, because we're on the top floor. Har-har." The man guffawed.

"No," said Nicky. "We just took the elevator up for a ride. I know there's not a thirteenth floor."

During the elevator ride down, Nicky thought about one of Grandma Zelda's stories. She had told him that many buildings in the city, like theirs, didn't have a thirteenth floor, because the thirteenth floor was considered unlucky. Sometimes tall buildings pretended they didn't have a thirteenth floor. They went from the twelfth floor to the fourteenth floor, but really the people that lived on the fourteenth floor lived on the thirteenth floor. They just acted like they didn't. Grandma Zelda said that the builder of the first building that called the thirteenth floor the thirteenth floor claimed luck would come to anyone who moved onto the thirteenth floor. A few folks paid premium prices and bought up all the apartments, then dared people to watch them thrive. Well, these sad souls would never gloat again. Within one year the dwellers of the apartments on the thirteenth floor had experienced divorce, disease, paralysis, bedbugs, mice, mites, dog bites, and bankruptcy. Nicky smiled thinking about Grandma Zelda's story. Lucy watched him and smiled too; she wasn't sure why.

The elevator door opened and the three passengers stepped out of the elevator and walked outside. The man with the dog turned to the right. Nicky and Lucy walked to the left, their long, thin shadows pointed back behind them toward the apartment building they had just left.

"I'll see you after school. Good luck finding your grandmother." Lucy held up the "Help me" note and they parted ways.

Brigadier-General Arnold

8:00 a.m.
Heading Downtown

Boys with backpacks walking alongside their briefcase-toting fathers passed Nicky on the left side and the right. The boys chatted away. They looked like they had a lot to talk about with their dads. Nicky couldn't imagine talking to his father like that.

He crossed on the green and walked toward Columbus Circle, where he'd take the 1 train downtown to South Ferry. Pigeon would be waiting for him there. They'd start searching for Grandma Zelda at the big-toe bottom of the city and work their way up. They wouldn't stop until they found her. Nicky could look low, along streets, under cars, in stores and restaurants, and down alleyways. Pigeon could search high; she'd look through windows and scan rooftops. Nicky didn't say anything to Pigeon, but he wanted to be the one who found Grandma Zelda. It wouldn't be bad if Pigeon found her, especially if she was stuck on the rooftop of a tall building or something like that, but if he could be the one who actually saw her first, he'd go over to her, tap her on the shoulder, and before she had a chance to see who it was, he'd throw his arms around her little body. Grandma Zelda was good at hugs. She was the only one in Nicky's family who ever hugged. She hugged so much that Nicky had started trying to escape from her hugs a few years back. These days when she hugged him, he stiffened his body like a piece of wood and stared ahead like a zombie. She'd tell him, "Loosen up, child. These arms have hugged more folks than I care to count. They've been wrapped around everyone from the great composer Igor Stravinsky to my favorite Ringling brother, Alfred, to Alan Klingensmith, that nice doorman from that building on Eighty-ninth Street and Riverside Drive. They've even hugged your father. And wouldn't you know it," she'd say, "not one of these fellows got cooties or head lice or any other varmint from one of my hugs."

After Nicky found Grandma Zelda, and after he gave her a giant hug, they'd get hot dogs for lunch and, thought Nicky, maybe stop by the Society Library to introduce Grandma Zelda to Lucy. Then Nicky could take Grandma Zelda back home, and she could bake a Zeldaberry pie for him. That would be king.

This was Nicky's first trip downtown. He hadn't been to too many places outside his neighborhood. His mother lived all the way in India, yet Nicky couldn't recall ever going below Forty-second Street. He went on a school trip to Philadelphia once, and to Bear Mountain, but he didn't remember what state it was in, maybe New Jersey or Delaware.

When Nicky reached the subway station on Fifty-ninth Street, he didn't give himself enough time for second thoughts before bounding down the stairs, two by two. A voice announced the approach of a downtown 1 train. Nicky ducked under a turnstile, pushed his way through the soapy-clean-smelling grown-ups, and found a spot on the train where he could stand in front of a subway map. When you had practice reading nautical maps, like Nicky did, subway maps were for babies. You didn't have to do anything but follow the red line, and Nicky had figured out his route before they'd reached the next stop.

On the way downtown the subway car sardine-stuffed with people, emptied out, sardine-stuffed again, and emptied out. The local stopped about every ten blocks, and before each stop the conductor announced the upcoming station. Nicky listened more carefully to the conductor than he ever did to his teachers at school.

By the time they announced his station, he had gotten a seat between two ladies who looked like sisters but didn't seem to know each other.

"Next stop, South Ferry," announced the conductor.

Nicky popped up and walked over to the sliding doors. He nodded a friendly hello to his reflection in the glass. He stuck out his tongue, pretended to get sick, and tried to look scary. When the doors opened, he was so busy chuckling to himself that he forgot about getting off. The *ding-ding* sounded again and the doors closed.

It's a good thing he knew how to read maps. The subway twisted and turned and barreled along. Nicky pushed his hands up against his ears, and then released them, to suction the screeching and howling sounds so that they sounded even more like a sick porpoise. Nicky was the only child aboard the entire train. He had no doubt that he'd find his way back to South Ferry. As soon as the doors opened again, he stepped off, ran across a platform, and long-jumped onto another train.

"Next stop, South Ferry," announced a voice.

No problem, he thought. After the doors opened, he got off, pushed his way upstairs through a small crowd, and started to run. He didn't stop until he saw Pigeon.

Downtown looked different. Smelled different too, more fishy and soupy. Did every zip code have its own smell? The zip code he lived in smelled normal. Well, normal but scented with Zeldaberry pie because of Grandma Zelda. After his mother left, Nicky used to wonder what her new house and her new street looked liked. He never thought about what it smelled like. For the first time Nicky wondered if his mother lived in an entirely different smell zone from him.

(When Mrs. Gibson moved to India two years ago, she told Nicky and Stella that some mothers take care of their children by helping them with their homework and feeding them, and others take care of them by leaving them, and that she was the other kind of mother. Neither Nicky nor Stella wanted the other kind of mother. Really, who would? The kind of mother they got didn't call, didn't e-mail, only sent an occasional postcard addressed to both of them. She had become the "Wish you were here"—but not really—kind of mother. It would have been a lie to say things had been fantastic before his mother had moved to India. The truth is, they weren't, but after she left, Nicky's father's dismal mood eroded even further. He pretty much stopped talking. He had never been terribly talkative, but after his wife's departure he pruned his already sparse use of words to the bare essentials, which seemed to be "You're in time-out" and a few other not-so-niceties. It seemed like he'd totally forgotten that phrases like "Great job, son" even existed.)

"I'd never know this was the city if I didn't know this was the city," said Nicky. Down here he felt like it was okay to talk to Pigeon. It was okay to do anything down here. "Let's go and find her. Smell for Zeldaberries."

Nicky flared his nostrils and pretended he was in a movie again. Pigeon followed along from the air. She looked through as many windows as possible. Each block had several boxy buildings, most of them filled with stacks and rows of windows. They were like waves; they just kept coming at her, one after another. She started skipping windows, then tried looking through two on a floor, then one on every other floor. Okay, five windows per block.

Fourteen blocks in, and still no Grandma Zelda. "Maybe I should ask around. Maybe someone has seen her," Nicky said.

Pigeon looked down the street. She saw a delivery boy on a bicycle, two ladies clip-clopped along in high heels, a man in a dark blue suit talked on his cell phone while he walked, and a man cloaked in rags leaned against the side of a building. Pigeon watched people every day and had learned that you never could tell what someone would do by the way they looked. Very nice-looking people weren't always very nice, and ratty-looking people didn't necessarily behave like rats.

"Not a good idea," said Pigeon. "Best not to talk to strangers. Don't forget you're just a boy."

Nicky, like every other child, had been warned about talking to strangers. He had never been given the exception to this rule, yet had been told many times that all rules have exceptions. Fathers want to play ball with their sons. His father, the exception. Mothers lived with their kids. His mother, the exception. And those were just two exceptions. Asking a stranger on the street about Grandma Zelda could be this rule's exception.

"I'll just ask two people. What if I walked by someone and didn't ask, and they'd seen Grandma Zelda? I'd never know it. I might spend the rest of my life looking for her, when the person I'd just walked by could have told me exactly where she was. You see, Pigeon? I really should ask."

"No," insisted Pigeon. "Absolutely not. No talking to strangers."

"How about just one?"

"Not even one."

"I talked to you. You're a stranger."

"I'm a pigeon. You're allowed to talk to strangers that are pigeons, dogs, cats, mice, rats, and squirrels. Though, I wouldn't bother talking to a sparrow. You'd get bored."

That was the exception to the rule—he could talk to animals. He should have figured.

A policeman turned onto their block and walked toward Nicky and Pigeon. Nicky could ask the policeman. Policemen were always exceptions. Except . . .

"Hey, Nicky," whispered Pigeon. "Can you get arrested for not going to school?"

11:10 a.m.

Nicky noticed right away that the policeman didn't have a red round face. Friendly policemen all had red round faces. This one had a long thin hot dog face and a big thick mustache, the type of mustache that looked like it wanted to be a beard. The policeman spotted Nicky watching him and made a move for his gun.

Nicky took off. Within seconds he heard the *slap-clap* of feet behind him. He zipped between

148

two parked cars and fled out into the street. A van swerved. A horn honked. He pushed his legs forward, but the *slap-clapping* caught up with him and—

Bang.

He was sure he heard a bang.

"Hey, kid. Stop running and turn around. Now!"

Better to stop than to get shot at again. Nicky slowly turned around, his eyes focused on the policeman's feet. He knew he should be looking up, at his face, but he kept his eyes glued to the polished black police shoes instead.

"What's your name, kid? And what kind of no good are you up to?" The policeman alternated words with deep huffing breaths.

"Nicky Gibson," he said. "I'm not doing anything, sir." *Maybe it wasn't a real bang,* thought Nicky. The bang was probably coming.

"Is that right?"

"Yes, sir," Nicky wondered if he should start crying.

"Then, why were you running from me?" asked the policeman.

"So you don't shoot me," replied Nicky.

"So I don't shoot you. I see," said the policeman. "You must have done something pretty terrible to think I'm going to shoot you."

"No, sir, but I saw you reach for your gun," said Nicky.

The policeman frowned. "My gun. I see. Could it have been this you saw me reaching for?" The policeman opened his right hand and revealed a tissue. "You took off like a kid who has gotten himself into big trouble. Should I have been reaching for my weapon? What kind of big trouble are you in?"

"None, sir."

"Then, tell me why you're not in school. How old are you, Nicky Gibson? Eight, nine?"

Nicky felt like lying with all his might but couldn't wrap his words around a lie to a policeman. "I'm eleven, sir. I'm short for my age. I maybe should be in school sir, but something important came up and I thought I better not go."

"I see," replied the policeman. "Big test? Forgot to do your homework?" The policeman tapped his foot.

"No, it's nothing like that."

If Nicky told the policeman about Grandma Zelda going missing, about the note, about everything that had happened, he could get help. With the entire New York City police force on the job, they'd find Grandma Zelda in an hour, tops, and the person who'd taken her would get arrested.

Put in jail.

Maybe for a long time.

That would be fine, unless his dad had something to do with Grandma Zelda's disappearance. It occurred to him that he'd do practically anything for proof that his dad had nothing to do with this. His dad might be mean, but he wasn't that bad. No father could be that bad, and if there were a father around somewhere who was that bad, it would be some other father, not his. So why did he even let himself start thinking about this? Of course his dad had nothing to do with Grandma Zelda going missing, but just in case, Nicky decided not to say anything to the policeman about it.

"Officer." Nicky lifted his head and looked into the policeman's eyes. "I cut school."

"I thought so. I'm going to take you in now," said the policeman.

Nicky stretched out his arms, wrists turned toward the sky, and closed his eyes.

"What are you doing?" asked the policeman.

"You can handcuff me," said Nicky. "I won't resist arrest."

"Sorry to disappoint you, son, but I'm taking you in to school, not the police station and not to jail."

12:05 p.m.
Balstonbridge School

Most days felt long, but on this day the first hour of school for Lucy seemed like two hours, the second hour seemed more like three hours, and the third hour, four. School lasted for seven hours, which meant that the last hour of school would feel like it lasted for eight hours, which is more than an entire school day in just one hour.

Lucy thought about Zelda's note. She tried to focus on what her teachers were saying, but today they all sounded like the teachers in Charlie Brown cartoons. "Whah, whah-whah, whah-whah."

During lunch period she sat with the ever-indecisive Caroline Minty and listened to her contemplate whether she should eat her meatballs before her mashed potatoes. She aired an impressive list of well-considered pros and cons, but in the end the mashed potatoes went first. Then Caroline Minty had the unenviable task of deciding whether she should have something healthy, like fruit, or less healthy, like pudding, for dessert.

While Caroline Minty rambled on, Lucy took Zelda's note out of her binder and laid it on her lunch tray. She could tell right away that the letters looked like they were written quickly and, given what the note said, under extreme duress—maybe at gunpoint, or knifepoint, or—who knew—penpoint. These letters had a lot more imperfections and jiggles in the lines than the letters in her other note. Lucy ached to take the light-up pocket magnifier out of her backpack but didn't feel like explaining to Caroline Minty everything that was going on.

It didn't matter. Caroline Minty noticed the note anyway. "What's that?"

"Just a note. A boy who lives in my building found it."

"Why do you have it, then?" asked Caroline Minty.

Lucy paused before answering. She watched Caroline Minty tuck a clump of hair behind her left ear. Her hair was already pulled back in a barrette on the other side. Lucy wanted to think of an answer that wouldn't lead to more questions. "He said I could borrow it for the day."

"Really? That's so cool. Can I see it? I mean, if that's okay with you. Is it okay with you? If it's not, that's okay too."

"Well, I probably shouldn't show it to anyone. Sorry." Lucy reached across her lunch tray to grab the note. That's when the only thing in the entire school day to happen quickly happened. Her hand accidentally smacked into her glass, and it toppled over, spilling water onto her tray and over the note.

"Oh, no," screeched Lucy.

"I'm so sorry. It was a mistake," apologized Caroline Minty. For a moment she even managed to confuse Lucy.

"What? What was a mistake?"

"I didn't mean to make you tip over the glass of water."

"You didn't. I don't know, maybe you did. It doesn't matter, but will you take my tray? Please, please, please?" begged Lucy. "I've got to try to save this note's life." She gently scraped the note off the plastic lunch tray, grabbed her backpack and binder, and headed to the second-floor girls' locker room to dry the note with a hair dryer.

12:20 p.m.

"You're kidding me," Lucy exclaimed. She jiggled the handle, but the door wouldn't open. She knocked loudly, but no one replied. Surely a custodian would walk by soon and unlock the door for her. It seemed like there were more custodians than students at this school. Everywhere you went someone was mopping. She looked up and down the hallway. The entire second floor seemed deserted. She peeked into the empty gymnasium and walked past empty offices. How could an entire floor of a school be empty in the middle of a school day? This, Lucy knew, would never happen back in Savannah. She had been waiting for what felt like an hour, but turned out to be four minutes, when Mrs. Costa walked by wiping her eyes.

"Lucy, what are you doing here?" she asked.

"I need to get into the locker room."

"Did you leave something in there? You kids are always leaving things behind. You'd never need to give a child who goes to this school bread crumbs for a walk in the forest, because every one of you leaves a trail of belongings behind as you go through the day."

Lucy didn't respond. She just nodded in agreement. Mrs. Costa's eyes looked pink. Lucy wondered if she had been crying. Probably, with all the terrible stuff going on in her life.

"I don't have a key to the locker room. You'll have to ask Ms. Swift for one and it doesn't look like she has a gym class at the moment."

"Thanks," said Lucy. She wanted to ask Mrs. Costa if she needed help with her terrible life, but it didn't seem like the right time to do that. So she didn't say anything and wouldn't have said anything if her father hadn't gotten out of the elevator.

"Lucy!" He looked at his watch. "Shouldn't you be finishing up with lunch and getting to your next class? Hello, Mrs. Costa."

"Hello, Mr. Bertel," replied Mrs. Costa. "Lucy left something in the locker room, but the door is locked."

"Oh, dear. What did you leave in there?" asked Mr. Bertel.

"Nothing, Dad. I just—"

"Lucy," said Mrs. Costa. "Don't fib to your father."

"I'm not," said Lucy. "I wasn't trying to get into the locker room because I left something in there."

"Lucy," said a sharp-tongued Mrs. Costa. "You told me you forgot something in there."

"I didn't."

"You shouldn't have lied to me."

"I didn't. I really didn't."

"Luc—"

"Mrs. Costa," interrupted Mr. Bertel. "I haven't seen you for a while. Is everything well with you?"

"Fine, just fine." She wiped her eyes. "Fine enough, I suppose. It's a bit of a tough time."

"Can we do anything to help?" asked Lucy.

Mrs. Costa looked a little startled and stumbled around with a few words before she figured out what to say. "Ah, belgo, humma, uma. Why don't you handle this situation with Lucy as you see fit, Mr. Bertel." Mrs. Costa stomped down the hallway into one of the empty offices.

Lucy shrugged her shoulders. "Dad," she said. "I need to use a hair dryer. An important piece of

evidence got wet, and I have to dry it right away."
Lucy was about to fill her father in on Zelda and the
mysterious note when the bell rang.

"Lucy-loo, lunch period is over. I'm afraid your
evidence will have to go to your next class soggy."
Mr. Bertel leaned over and kissed Lucy on the top
of her head. "Hurry up, off to class."

3:05 p.m.
The Society Library, East Seventy-ninth Street

Lucy paced the length of the awning outside the
Society Library. She didn't know how to tell Nicky
about the note. While she waited for him, she tried
out different approaches.

"Nicky, I have some bad news. . . . Nicky,
remember the note from your grandmother? Well,
something unexpected happened. . . . Nicky, do you
believe accidents happen for a reason? . . . Nicky,
I'm so sorry. You can make as much noise as you
want and I'll never think bad thoughts about you
again. I promise."

By the time Lucy figured out that he wasn't
going to show up, she had thought of sixty-two
ways to apologize for the wet note.

Way number sixty-two, her final apology, sounded like this:

"Nicky, you're annoying and you don't deserve my help. Here's the note from your grandmother. It got ruined."

In twenty-two minutes her dad would want to go home and get dinner ready. *What a wasted day,* thought Lucy. Of all the apartments to live in, why did her family have to pick the one underneath the most annoying boy in all of New York City? It sometimes felt like nothing had worked out for her since they moved.

Lucy checked her watch one last time, then headed inside. She looked back at the entrance to the library door twice before she reached the circulation desk. *Forget him,* she thought. *He'll have to find his grandmother without me.*

5:00 p.m.
Crosstown Bus

On the bus ride home Lucy texted the Wrighties about Nicky, the "Help me" note, and Nicky not showing up. She hadn't talked to them for a long time and felt bad about not returning a bunch of texts, but right now she desperately needed someone other than a parent or a pigeon to talk to. She needed people who would understand exactly how annoying Nicky was. People who could feel bad for her.

They texted back right away:

> Omg what if he was kidnapped?
> Or killed????
> Or hit by a car!!!
> R u scared 4 him?
> What r u going 2 do?
> U have 2 missing ppl
> U need 2 find Nicky!
> And his grandma!

So much for understanding. They did have a point though. It's not good for a family to have two people missing at once. She better find one of them, at the very least.

Once back in their building, a building that probably had two fewer people in it than it should, Lucy picked up her father's large hand and placed it between her two smaller ones. "Dad," she said in her most grown-upy voice, "I've got something to do that doesn't involve you. Nothing personal. I won't be long. You go on home without me."

"Sounds intriguing, Lucy-loo." said her father.

5:30 p.m.
West 66th Street, Apartment 7D

Lucy got out of the elevator on the seventh floor. The hallway was painted an icy shade of blue. The hallway on the sixth floor, where she lived, had much prettier gold-and-red-striped wallpaper. She stood in front of apartment 7D and looked at the name printed on the door. GIBSON. She put her finger on the doorbell but didn't push down.

Instead she inhaled a yoga breath. If Nicky's mom or dad answered, she'd say she was new to the building and wondered if Nicky was home. If they said they hadn't seen him all day, she'd ask when was the last time they'd heard from him. If they said not since this morning, she'd sit them down and tell them that Nicky had cut school in order to find his grandmother, and she'd ask them for handwriting samples. She pushed her finger down on the doorbell. *Ding-dong.*

Lucy heard footsteps coming toward the door.

"Who's there?" It was a girl's voice. Lucy hadn't been prepared for that possibility.

"It's Lucy. I live downstairs."

Nicky's sister, Stella, opened the door. Lucy had shared a few elevator rides with Stella, but Stella always had headphones on, so they'd never talked.

"Hi. I live downstairs," she repeated.

"I know," said Stella.

"Is Nicky home?"

Stella smiled and laughed. "You want to see my brother?" she asked, clearly surprised. Stella had never thought a girl, especially a pretty girl like Lucy, might want to talk to her brother. "Are you sure you're in the right place?"

"I'm sure. Is Nicky home, or did he—"

"NICKY," Stella called out. "SOME GIRL IS HERE FOR YOU."

"Lucy. My name's Lucy."

"NICKY. LUCY IS HERE FOR YOU."

"So he's home. He's been home all along?" asked Lucy. She spoke very slowly, "You know, maybe I don't need to see him."

"Yup," replied Stella. "That's what I expected. Do you know that dork cut every class he had this morning? He gets in trouble with our dad for breathing. For doing something this bad and getting caught by the police, he's never, ever going to see the light of day again. You almost gotta feel bad for the guy."

"Yeah, I guess," said Lucy. "Actually, I do want to see him."

"He's probably not coming out of his room because my dad tied him to his bed or something."

"Really? Your dad would do that?"

"Well." Stella reconsidered. "He probably wouldn't go that far, but boy, was he red-hot mad. He's not home now, so it's safe to come in if you want to see Nicky. Trust me, I understand why you wouldn't, if you don't."

"Is your mom home?" asked Lucy.

"No," replied Stella. "She hasn't been home for two years."

"Oh." Lucy looked down at the floor. "I think I will come in."

Stella popped her head into Nicky's room. "You have a visitor. I don't think you've ever had a visitor. This is, like, world news."

"You're so funny I almost forgot to—"

Stella opened Nicky's door wide enough for him to see Lucy and continued her not-funny-at-all stand-up comedy act. "A friend. Wow. Where have I been? Mars, I guess. The last time I looked, you had fewer friends than a skunk."

Nicky looked at Lucy's big eyes and remembered that he was supposed to have met up with her after school. "Sorry I couldn't go to the library today."

"That's okay. I wasn't really expecting you," said Lucy.

"I kind of got in trouble," said Nicky.

"Yeah, I heard that. Can I come in?" Lucy stepped inside Nicky's room and closed his door before he had a chance to answer.

"Actually, I'm on my way out. I have to go upstairs before my father gets home. Hopefully my grandmother is back at home."

"Hopefully," said Lucy. "I have your note, but, well, you see . . ." She paused. "Would it be okay if I came with you?"

"I guess," said Nicky. "But we have to go this minute. I'm supposed to be in a time-out, and I don't want my sister to know I'm leaving, because she'll tell on me. Can you go right now?"

"I'm ready," said Lucy. She hadn't even sat down. She had barely taken two steps into his room. She could leave as quickly as she'd arrived. She reached out her arm and opened the door. Stella's ear—well, her whole body—had been pressed up against the other side of the door, and when the door opened, she came tumbling in.

"Oops. Sorry. Just walking by and the door opened. The indraft must have sucked me in," said Stella. She straightened out her shirt and stood up.

"Is Dad back?" asked Nicky.

"Not yet," said Stella.

"Promise you won't tell him if I go out for just a minute."

"No, I don't. It's my fiduciary duty as your older sister to tell on you," said Stella.

"Whatever," said Nicky. "Just please don't be fiduciary for five minutes. Then you can fidute again all you want."

"All right," agreed Stella, pretty much because she had no idea what "fiduciary" or "fidute" meant. She just knew they sounded important, and she liked to show off her vocabulary to strangers.

Nicky grabbed Lucy's arm before she reached the elevator and pulled her into the back stairwell. "Just in case my father's in the elevator. It's safer this way," he said.

They ran up six steps. Then Nicky turned around.

"Can you do this?"

He jumped.

"Probably," said Lucy. "I thought you were in a rush."

"Oh, yeah. I am," said Nicky. "But jump first."

"What?" It didn't make sense to waste time on jumping. "No."

"Come on," said Nicky. "Just once. It won't take but a second."

"You're kidding, right?" Now Lucy understood. Nicky had a jumping problem. He couldn't do anything without jumping. She'd moved eight hundred miles and had ended up living under a boy with a jumping problem. Talk about unfair. "I don't want to."

"Are you scared?" asked Nicky. "Just pretend you're flying."

"Are you crazy?" said Lucy.

"Just one jump. Please," begged Nicky.

Lucy looked at his floppy orange hair and pleading blue eyes and decided that the two of them would probably never get to his grandmother's house if she didn't jump.

"Fine," she said. "I'll jump. But only once." She stood on the sixth step and looked down to the landing below. It looked farther away than she'd expected. Four steps seemed like a reasonable number to jump. Only someone who had jumping issues would want to jump from the sixth step. She closed her eyes, bent her knees, took a breath, and jumped.

"OWWY! Ow! My ankle!"

5:45 p.m.
West 68th Street, Stairwell

"Are you okay?"

"Ouch!" Lucy cried out.

"Be quiet," Nicky warned. "Someone will hear you. Why'd you close your eyes?"

"Why'd you make me jump?" Lucy's words sputtered out through clenched teeth.

"I didn't make you. I thought you'd want to. It's fun if you know how to do it right."

"Owww." She tried to rub the pain out of her ankle, but it just got worse. She thought about yelling so she wouldn't cry but bit down on her bottom lip instead.

"Is it broken?" asked Nicky.

"I don't know. I think it's okay. Can you help me up or something?"

Lucy stretched out her arms. Nicky grabbed her around the waist, entirely ignoring her outstretched arms, and hoisted her up. "Can you walk?" he asked.

She stepped down on her right foot and felt sparks scrambling around in her leg. "Yeah, but it hurts. Can we just go upstairs and stop talking about it?"

"Should I carry you?" asked Nicky.

"What?" Lucy looked at Nicky and suddenly felt like a flamingo standing, on one long thin leg, next to a wide little duck. "Um, I don't think so."

Lucy grasped on to the banister and hauled herself up step by step. Once they made it to the eighth floor, Nicky noticed right away that Grandma Zelda's doorknob still hadn't been replaced. He pushed the apartment door open.

"Wow," Lucy said as she entered Grandma

Zelda's apartment. It's not that she cared about the many paintings and photographs on the wall; she didn't. It's not that she liked the bright red paint; she didn't. Lucy had spotted a stack of envelopes with handwritten addresses. "This place is amazing."

Grandma Zelda's kitchen smelled strikingly similar to Nicky's odorless one. He made the connection as soon as his nose filled with the scent of emptiness—a bad sign if ever there was one. Nicky walked into the bedroom. "Grandma Zelda, are you here?" he called out. He checked the bathroom— "Grandma Zelda?"—and a small walk-in closet, to make certain she hadn't gotten lost behind the racks of clothing. "She's not here."

Lucy's internal radar led her directly to a desk covered with notes, letters, and official-looking documents. She wiped her hands on her pants and then picked up a piece of lined paper filled, from top to bottom, with beautiful, glorious old-fashioned handwriting. She started breathing faster and forgot about the pain in her ankle. "Nicky, do you think I can take some of these papers. I promise I'll give them back."

"I guess," said Nicky. "It's not like my grandmother is here to use them. I don't know why you want all that junk, though."

Lucy frowned and shook her head. What could you expect from a jumping maniac head-stomper? "What are you going to do now?" she asked.

"I wish I knew," Nicky replied. "I've never had a missing grandmother before."

Lucy held up the pile of paper. "Maybe there are clues in here about what happened to her."

Nicky thought about Grandma Zelda's two notes and realized there might be more. "Do you need help carrying that? You know, with your ankle and everything?" He paused. "Wait. Shhh. Did you hear that?" he asked.

Lucy heard a lady's voice followed by a kind of half roar, half voice. "Is that your—"

Nicky lunged forward and grabbed Lucy by the waist, now for the second time, and dragged her into Grandma Zelda's closet.

"What are you—"

He planted his hand smack across her mouth. "Shhh," he whispered. "Don't say anything."

Nicky ripped all of Grandma Zelda's clothes

off their hangers and dumped them onto the floor. "Hide under these."

Lucy clutched on to Grandma Zelda's papers. Nicky closed the closet door and dove into the heap of clothing. "Come on," he said.

"Okay. Is there enough room?"

"Yeah, but hurry. Put these over your head."

"Can you see me?"

"No. Can you see me?"

"No."

"Ouch. You're on my ankle."

"Sorry." Nicky rotated his body and draped a robe over his head.

"Why are we hiding?" whispered Lucy.

"I'll explain everything later," said Nicky.

The closet door swung open. Nicky held his breath and shut his eyes. Lucy grabbed on to something and squeezed it, trying desperately not to cough or sneeze or burp or hiccup. She didn't realize, at first, that the thing she had grabbed was Nicky's hand.

"Oh, my shooting stars. I'm sincerely shocked by this monstrous mountain of a mess." It was the same lady's voice they had heard in the other room.

Nicky recognized his father's voice immediately. "We'll have that emptied out in no time."

Then a third voice that neither of them recognized, "The entire apartment will need to be emptied before I'd even consider moving in."

Mr. Gibson again: "It's all going to the dump. Come back for a look next week. I can assure you, everything will be cleaned out of here."

Nicky squeezed Lucy's hand. She felt bad for him, so she squeezed back. They heard the patter of continued apologies being made, then the slam of a door.

"Was that the front door?" asked Lucy.

"I think so," said Nicky. He opened his eyes and stood up. "I don't hear anyone. Let's get out of here. I'm supposed to be in a time-out. I've got to get home before my father figures out I'm not in my room."

Lucy struggled to get up. A yellow dress hung from her head and a pink satiny robe was draped over her shoulders like a boa.

"But what about your grandmother? You don't know anything yet. What about all of this?" Lucy held out the stack of papers. "You can't go home. We need to find out what happened to your grandmother."

Nicky tried not to laugh at the sight of Lucy's giant eyes peeking out from under Grandma Zelda's dress. He didn't want her to think he was laughing at her after they had held hands. He had never held hands with a girl who had a dress on her head before. For that matter, he had never held any girl's hand.

"We should read these," said Lucy. "Do you know who those people were or what they wanted?"

"The loud one was my dad. It sounds like he's about to empty out Grandma Zelda's apartment. I wish I knew what was going on. I do know that as soon as my father figures out that I'm not in my room, I'll probably be put in time-out for the rest of my life, and my afterlife. I haven't even decided if I believe in an afterlife, but if there is one, I'm sure I'll be spending it in a time-out," said Nicky.

"Then it doesn't matter," said Lucy. "I think your grandmother needs us."

"I know she does," said Nicky. He glanced at Grandma Zelda's viola d'amore, which was resting on her bed, on the spot where she should have been taking a nap.

6:15 p.m.
Apartment 6D

"Sign this contract." Lucy pulled a piece of paper out of her inkjet printer and placed it in front of Nicky.

Rules and Regulations
Case #001: Zelda Gibson—Missing Grandmother
1. No jumping at any time.
2. Hands must be clean and dry before handling any and all documents.
3. Don't throw anything away. Everything is important. Even things that don't look important are important.
I agree now, and forevermore, herein and here out, in this life and any afterlife, if there is one or not, to abide by the rules and regulations as outlined above and signed below.

X: _____
Nicky Gibson

X: _____
Lucy Bertel

Nicky scanned the words without really reading them. He recognized each one individually, just not grouped together. He grabbed a pen and signed his name.

x: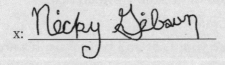

"Wow," said Lucy. Her eyes looked larger than usual. Since Lucy's eyes played such a prominent role on her face, people often neglected to look at her nose, mouth and cheeks. Lucy's long dark hair was her second most noticeable feature. The rest of her looked like a typical pretty eleven-year-old girl.

"Oh, my gosh!"

"What did I do wrong?" asked Nicky.

"Other than your *i* and *o*, nothing."

"What about my *i* and *o*?" Nicky suddenly felt the urge to protect his letters. He grabbed the contract from Lucy and double-checked his *i* and *o*. They looked like every *i* and *o* he had ever written. (True, his teachers constantly told him to write more legibly, but they never mentioned a problem with either his *i* or his *o*, and by the time you're in sixth grade, if you had an *i* or *o* problem, someone would have mentioned it.) "There's nothing wrong with them."

"Your *is* are *os* and your *os* are *us*, explained Lucy. "You didn't know you do that?"

"Do what?"

"Make your *is os* and your *os us*. It's not such a bad thing. I mean, I'd trust a kid with an open *o* a lot more than one who has his *o* all tangled up at the top. Wouldn't you?"

LWR #10: IF YOU TIE A BOW IN YOUR O, THERE ARE THINGS YOU DON'T WANT PEOPLE TO KNOW.

Spinning in place, that's the only way to describe how Nicky's brain felt. He spoke in whole words, and Lucy talked in letters. She'd be making more sense if she spoke Mandarin. At least he took that language in school.

"You really ought to see this," she said.

Nicky looked out Lucy's window. Her view should have been the same as his, but strangely, being one floor down changed how everything looked. He wondered where Pigeon had gone. Hopefully she was still searching for Grandma Zelda. He looked back at the door and thought about what kind of bad mood his father would be in if he went home. His options seemed dismally limited at the moment. On the one hand, there was Lucy and her letters, and on the other, there was Nicky's father and his time-outs. Nicky shut his eyes and wished with all his might that when he opened them his arms would have turned into long feathery wings. If only he could fly.

"Look at the difference between your 'Gibson' and your grandmother's 'Gibson.' Think about it. You're two people with the same name from the same family, but you have two entirely different ways of signing your name. And I bet your dad and sister's 'Gibson's look nothing like either of these 'Gibson's.'"

"I know my sister's doesn't. Her signature looks like she lost control of a Spiro-graph."

Lucy laughed. She didn't know Stella but could

have guessed that she'd embellish her signature with a lot of extra loops and circles and curlicues. Lucy pulled Nicky over to her desk and pointed to something that looked like a lamp and lit up like a lamp but was actually a magnifying glass, not a lamp. He leaned over it and looked through a large round convex piece of glass at Grandma Zelda's flowing letters. "I see it now. There's no way that *i* is anything other than an *i*, and her *o* looks exactly like an *o* to me," he said. "But she's not a kid. She's had practically a hundred years to practice her *i*s and *o*s. Maybe she had an *i o u* problem when she was a kid. Why do you have all this stuff, anyway?" Nicky pointed to the microscopes, magnifying glasses, air blowers, inks, toothpicks, and compasses on her desk.

"To study handwriting," said Lucy.

"For what?"

"To know about people and solve crimes," explained Lucy. "There is evidence in every letter. Any criminal who uses a pen better watch out for me."

"Well, I don't like to write," confessed Nicky. "So you'll never catch me when I commit a crime."

"I already know that your *is* are *o*s and your *o*s are *u*s, so you're as good as caught. What crime are you going to commit, anyway? Do you think you'll be a thief?"

"I don't know," said Nicky. "I want to be a sailor. There's not a lot of stealing you can do when you're out in the middle of the ocean, unless you're a pirate, but I don't like wearing eye patches too much."

"So you don't want to be a pirate, then?" asked Lucy.

"Naw, I just want to sail. Maybe I'll join the navy," said Nicky. "Have you solved any crimes yet? Or is my missing grandmother your first big case?"

"First big case" made her sound official. Maybe there were worse things in the world than being a head-stomper. At least his *o* was a sign that he was open-minded. Lucy noticed the time. 6:26. "Do you want to have dinner with us?" she asked.

6:30 p.m.

Nicky sat down for dinner with the Bertels and the world got small. Suddenly only two places existed—his apartment building on Sixty-eighth

Street and India. Even though Nicky had been told that India was a large country, he thought of it as about the size of his hand. That's how big it was in the atlas. When he thought about his mom living there, he envisioned her as a tiny ant-size person, someone who could have a house and a car and an entire life that fit on the knuckle of his pointer finger.

"I hope you like Indian food," said Dr. Bertel.

"I do," Nicky said. He had never tasted Indian food before, but if it tasted like it smelled, he figured he'd like it. "My mom lives in India," said Nicky.

"Well, what do you know," said Mr. Bertel. "My folks live in India as well."

"And my great-grandma," added Lucy.

"That's right," agreed Dr. Bertel. "My grandmother is outside of Mumbai. Where does your mother live?"

"Someplace called Pune." The Bertels' kitchen smelled delicious. Different from Zeldaberry-pie delicious and different from the usual delicious smells that Nicky knew, but still delicious. Their kitchen had orange clay tiles on the floor. The cabinets, refrigerator, and even the dishwasher were made out of wood. At least that's how it looked. Nicky's refrigerator was white with rust stains dripping down the front, the dishwasher was black, and the floor was speckled with gummy spots that made your socks stick to it.

"What a surprise. Our families are practically neighbors. Have you been there to visit?" asked Dr. Bertel.

Nicky eyes grazed his plate. "No." He didn't like to talk about his mom too much. What was the point? He also felt a little ashamed that his mom hadn't asked him and Stella to visit her. He didn't know if people would think she was a bad mom or they were bad kids. Either way, it was embarrassing.

"Nicky, may I serve you? Why don't you try the Samosas and puri first?" Mr. Bertel spooned two large dumpling-like things and a light brown bread balloon onto Nicky's plate.

"Thank you," said Nicky.

"I have an ethical question," said Lucy, jumping right in. "Is it okay to read someone else's personal letters if they're not around?"

"Where are they?" asked Mr. Bertel.

"I don't know, just not around," answered Lucy.

"'Not around,' like they've run out to the store to get milk?"

"Sure," said Lucy.

"I would say no, then."

"What about if you want to study their handwriting?" asked Lucy.

"They would need to grant you permission," said Dr. Bertel. "I've found you really shouldn't do anything these days without getting permission."

"What do you think, Lucy?" asked Mr. Bertel.

"I think all handwriting should be available to be studied."

"Nicky, would you like someone looking at your handwriting without your knowledge?"

"I don't write."

"Oh, of course you don't," said Dr. Bertel. "Handwriting has become a lost art in this age of computers."

Nicky finished his Samosas and filled his plate with rice and chicken tandoori. Lucy had taken only two bites. She had a point to make and couldn't be bothered with eating until everyone agreed with her.

"That's why it's very important to study handwriting. It's going extinct."

Nicky added, "Maybe writing should be put in the witness protection program."

Everyone laughed but Nicky. "Um, I think you meant to say it should be protected by the Endangered Species Act," said Lucy. She arched her eyebrows and looked at Nicky.

He shook his head. "No. I think if more endangered species were in the witness protection program, they probably wouldn't be so endangered."

"You know," said Mr. Bertel, "the boy has a point."

"I say we start a witness protection program to save the letters that are in danger of going extinct," proposed Lucy.

"Good plan," said Dr. Bertel. "I can think of a bunch of cursive letters that should gain immediate access."

"Save the letters!" called out Lucy. "We'll start an organization. It'll be called SHWI, for Save Handwriting Immediately, and we'll make posters and talk to Congress and the president, and everyone will pick up a pen and start to write." Lucy glanced over at Nicky. His lips looked yellow, so she smiled at him.

"Indian food is king. It's really good," he said, and smiled back.

7:05 p.m.

Nicky and Lucy spent the following half hour separating Grandma Zelda's papers into piles. Lucy handed Nicky one pile and asked him to read every word, no skipping. She brought a second, larger pile, over to her desk and pulled out a half-dollar-size magnifying glass—the same kind that jewelers use to check if a diamond is real or a fake. That's when the doorbell rang.

From inside Lucy's room Nicky heard the unmistakable roar. "Is my son here?" Stella had told on him, after all. Actually, it was surprising it had taken this long.

Lucy quickly covered Grandma Zelda's papers, so that Mr. Gibson wouldn't see them if he came in.

"Should I hide?" asked Nicky.

"No," said Lucy. "My parents will kill me if they think I'm harboring a time-out fugitive. You'd better surrender. I'll keep working. We'll find your grandmother."

Nicky looked over at her and the pile of

Grandma Zelda's papers. "I owe you," he said, and rushed to the front door.

"Hi, Dad. I can explain." Then he turned to Mr. Bertel. "Thank you for dinner."

Mr. Bertel replied with, "Nice to meet you. I hope we get to spend some time together again." Mr. Bertel had enough experience as a father and a teacher to know that the immediate future didn't look good for Nicky. When fathers have to run around ringing doorbells to find sons, it's never a good sign. The boy seemed polite and nice enough, thought Mr. Bertel. Hopefully whatever punishment he got wouldn't be too devastating.

7:40 p.m.
Apartment 7D

"Am I in time-out?" asked Nicky.

"No," replied Mr. Gibson.

NO? Had he just heard the word "no"? Nicky stopped inhaling midbreath to process. Could this be an April Fools' Day trick? April Fools had been yesterday. This looked like his dad standing over him. Other dads looked more—well, simply put, dadlike. They wore baseball caps and sneakers and T-shirts and colors other than gray.

"What did you tell them?" Mr. Gibson stared at the wall in front of him.

"Who?" replied Nicky. He tried to catch his father's eye.

"Did you say anything?" asked Mr. Gibson, still not looking at Nicky.

"About what?" Nicky checked the window. Seemed strange, but he kind of wanted a time-out. Not one of those marathon double-header time-outs. Just a short one to give him a moment to think about everything that had happened and to update Pigeon. Where was Pigeon, anyway? He hadn't seen her since before the police car ride.

Mr. Gibson sat on the corner of Nicky's bed. The mattress sunk down, and Nicky looked down upon his father. He stood up on his tiptoes to gain another inch and a half. He took a deep breath and summoned his courage. If his father got angry at him and yelled and put him in a time-out, so what? He was always in time-out. It didn't matter if he made his dad mad. What mattered was finding out what had happened to Grandma Zelda. "Do you mean did I tell them that Grandma Zelda is gone and you haven't done anything about it? Did I tell them you are taking all her stuff and dumping it in the trash? And that you don't even care about where she is? Or that something terrible probably happened to the nicest person alive and you don't care? Is that what you mean? Did I tell them all of that?"

Mr. Gibson picked up Nicky's stuffed dolphin by his dorsal fin and spun it around. He didn't answer Nicky's questions. Instead he started talking about the strange summerlike weather and the full moon and how sometimes unexpected weather makes people do inexplicable and unimaginable things.

Mr. Gibson hadn't talked this much to Nicky in more than a year, and for a moment, listening to his father, Nicky felt lucky. He pinched himself. That's what you're supposed to do when you think you might be in a dream. His pinch didn't hurt, but he knew deep down he wasn't dreaming, so it didn't matter. Perhaps now he could find out the truth about what had happened to his grandmother. Perhaps now he and his dad could sit down and really talk.

"What does the weather or the moon have to

do with Grandma Zelda?" asked Nicky. "Dad, we need to find out what happened to her." Nicky had a fleeting thought. Maybe they could find her together. Nicky and his dad and Lucy would team up and solve the mystery of Grandma Zelda.

Unlikely.

Mr. Gibson cleared his throat with a thunderous crackle and stood up. "Nicky, your grandmother can handle whatever comes her way. She's had a life of adventures. I don't think that ends because you get older. It's best if you don't worry about her. Sometimes things happen because they need to happen. Some ends justify the means. Sometimes things are complicated. I'm sure you'll understand when you get older."

"But, Dad—" As all kids know, conversations end as soon as the "You'll understand when you get older" line gets used. What adults never seem to realize is that when you get older you forget how to understand.

Mr. Gibson stood up and walked to the door. "Enough questions." He left the room. Conversation over. Nicky pinched himself again. He still didn't feel a thing.

PART SIX

"Where have you been?" asked Nicky.

"Looking for your grandmother," said Pigeon. "I searched until the sun fell behind the river. I started again at five thirty this morning. She's not an easy person to find. Six times I thought I saw her; six times I was wrong. I'm on my way uptown and stopped by for an update. How was jail?"

"I didn't go to jail." Nicky and Pigeon both looked at the metal bars on his window and shared a thought. There are jails and there are jails. "Grandma Zelda being gone stinks worse than sewage. I don't have school today. I'll help you look again," offered Nicky.

Pigeon bobbed her head and paced the length of Nicky's windowsill. "I'm not sure I can handle that. This is stressful enough without—" Before Pigeon had a chance to finish her sentence, Mr. Gibson barged into Nicky's room.

"I've got a meeting this morning, and I don't want you sneaking out of the house again, so I'm putting you in time-out."

Mr. Gibson looked like an overcast day. His

skin had turned a light shade of gray, which, Pigeon thought, nicely matched the rest of his outfit. In his left hand Mr. Gibson held an empty suitcase, and in his right, a manila folder. By the way he was leaning to the right, it looked like the folder weighed more than the suitcase.

"Why do you have a suitcase? Are you leaving too?" asked Nicky.

Mr. Gibson never believed that paternal duty included explaining things to his children, so Nicky's and Stella's questions generally remained unanswered. He clearly had no intention of answering this question either. Nicky knew that. Why bother asking? Waste of breath.

Pigeon, still on the windowsill, fanned out her wings. A feather popped out and drifted into Nicky's room, landing on Mr. Gibson left foot. "Disgusting," Mr. Gibson grumbled. He looked out Nicky's window and barked, "Close that window. There's a pigeon out there. Those things are nothing but rats with wings. Never mind. I'll do it. That way it will get done."

The suitcase fell from his hand. He placed the manila folder on the radiator and thrust his arms out toward Pigeon. After slamming the window shut, Mr. Gibson picked up the suitcase. On his way out he reminded Nicky of something he needed no reminder of. "Don't forget, you're in time-out."

"I won't. It's hard to forget my life," mumbled Nicky.

Nicky stood on his bed, bounced a few times, and then jumped off, flapping his arms and plummeting down to the floor. He hopped on one foot over to his window and opened it as wide as it would go, but Pigeon was already long gone. He picked up the folder. He thought about calling out for his father and telling him he had forgotten it, but he quickly reconsidered and decided instead to toss it out the window. No, he'd make paper airplanes with the papers in it and send them flying across the street. Nicky removed the top page from a small pile of documents in the folder and folded it in half.

He creased the corner and noticed Grandma Zelda's name, so he unfolded the paper. *Transfer of Ownership Deed* was typed in bold letters at the top of the page. Nicky read a bunch of words about how "I, Zelda Gibson, agree to," followed by a bunch of big words, "transfer ownership to Peter Gibson," then another bunch of big words with a bunch of other words. At the bottom of the page next to an *x:*, Grandma Zelda had signed her name.

Nicky looked at the signature, examining her perfect *i* and *o*, which didn't look perfect at all.

"Wait one minute," he said out loud.

9:50 a.m.
Apartment 6D

"Hi again," said Nicky. "Is Lucy home?"

Mr. Bertel was pleased to see that Nicky appeared to be in reasonably good shape. He seemed to be missing his shoes and his hair was bit less mussed than before. "Why don't you come in, and I'll see if she's available."

Nicky stepped inside the apartment while Mr. Bertel walked down the hallway to Lucy's bedroom and knocked on her door. "Lucy, you have a visitor. Are you free, or should I send him packing?"

"I'm in the middle of a . . . Who is it?" she asked. (Occasionally Caroline Minty stopped by unexpectedly. She was usually on her way somewhere else but changed her mind about going and asked her mom, or whoever was shuttling her around, if they could stop by Lucy's house and see if she wanted to hang out.)

"It's Nicky," said Mr. Bertel.

"Tell him to come in. I've got something to show him."

Lucy noticed Nicky's socks immediately. "Did you run away?" she asked.

"I'm not sure," he said. He looked at his socks and saw that his big toe had popped out of a hole. "I have something that I need you to look at." He handed Lucy the transfer of ownership deed.

"Do you know what this is?" asked Lucy.

"It's a transfer of ownership deed, whatever that means. My father left it in my room. My grandmother signed it. Look at her signature. Her *i* looks like an *o* and her *o* has a knot on top."

Lucy placed the deed under the big magnifying glass and focused on each letter for a full minute. She didn't say a word for eleven minutes. During this quiet time Nicky poked around Lucy's room. Even though it was directly under his room, and the same size and shape as his, it felt completely different. She had a LUCY'S LABORATORY sign above her desk and filing cabinets everywhere. Nicky had never known of a kid who had so much stuff to file. All his papers fit in a box under his bed. He opened one of the drawers and couldn't believe how many rows of files she had. It was like she was a grown-up or something. He pulled out a folder labeled *Napoléon Bonaparte*.

"Cool," said Nicky. "Why do you have a Napoléon Bonaparte file?"

Lucy didn't answer for a few minutes. Without lifting her head she finally responded, "I collect his signatures. You can find a lot of them online. Napoleon changed the way he signed his name all the time. Some people change their signature for different things they do or at different times in their lives."

LWR #11: DIFFERENT SIGNS FOR DIFFERENT TIMES.

Nicky wondered why Napoléon Bonaparte, the emperor of France, someone who could do anything he wanted, would ever choose to sign his name. If Nicky were emperor, he wouldn't do any writing.

"Maybe my grandmother is pulling a Napoléon," joked Nicky.

"No," said Lucy. "Her signature looks different here because she didn't sign this. At least I'm pretty sure she didn't. Someone wanted it to look like she signed it. They didn't do a totally terrible job, but they definitely weren't a professional. Do you know who would forge her name?" Lucy looked directly into Nicky's eyes. "Well, do you?"

"Is it illegal to sign someone else's name?" Nicky asked.

"Kind of, yes."

"Do you know what a transfer of ownership deed is?" asked Nicky.

"I'm pretty sure this says that your grandmother gave your father her apartment."

Nicky didn't say anything.

"Nice gift," said Lucy, before adding, "if it really was a gift."

Nicky noticed that his baby toe was sticking out of his sock too. "I can guess who did it, but I'm not sure I want to tell you."

Nicky had left his keys upstairs, in the side pocket of the backpack he had hidden under his bed. "Maybe my sister is home," he said. "Otherwise we're doomed."

They rang the doorbell. After a long delay and more ringing, Stella answered "You two are at it again. Didn't you learn anything from yesterday?"

"Stella," Nicky said, "I'm not kidding around. There's something important you should know."

Nicky and Lucy spent the next twenty minutes telling Stella about everything that had happened since Nicky had discovered that Grandma Zelda had gone missing. At first Stella accused them of concocting a story so she wouldn't squeal on them again. If given the chance to believe Nicky or not, she'd choose *not* out of habit. She hadn't factored Lucy in, though, and something about the way Lucy talked made her seem honest. Also, Stella would do almost anything to have eyes as big as Lucy's, even believe this ridiculous tale. Maybe if she spent time with Lucy she'd find out how Lucy got her eyes to look so big.

"Stella, I have a plan," Lucy said. "But for it to work I'll need to look through some of your father's papers."

"Bad idea," said Stella. "Anyway, he'll be back home soon."

Lucy put her hand on Stella's shoulder and tried to reassure her. "I'll be fast. We need your help. We need to do this now. Who knows what will happen to your grandmother if we don't figure out what's going on soon?"

"I don't know about this," said Stella. "Do you know how much trouble we'll all get in if he finds out somebody's been in his stuff?"

"If he has nothing to hide, your dad will never know we were in his stuff."

Nicky felt his stomach flop. "Can we get this over with now? I'm not feeling so well."

"All right," said Stella. "But I still don't think it's a good idea. I'll show you his office first."

"Whatever you do, no matter what, even if there's a tornado or a national emergency, you can't let your dad back into the apartment while I'm working."

"We won't. I've got the door covered. There's

no way he can get in," said Nicky. "But hurry up anyway."

Stella led Lucy into Mr. Gibson's office. "Are you certain you know what you're doing? My dad never lets anyone into his office. I can't believe I am involved in this."

"Maybe you shouldn't come in here with me," said Lucy.

"Okay," agreed Stella. "Only, don't make a mess. Don't touch anything."

"Don't worry." Lucy tried to sound reassuring. "Make sure you and Nicky don't let him back into the apartment, though. No matter what. Okay?"

Stella gulped loudly, and Lucy walked through the door into Mr. Gibson's office.

The first strange thing she noticed was his desk. It had a computer, which was turned off; a printer; a telephone; and a wire cup holding three pencils and two pens. She settled into a chair and stared at a desk so meticulously clean that it looked brand-new. The room looked like it had been stripped of clues about what Mr. Gibson did for work. He didn't seem to do anything that required files or notes or much of anything at all.

She hated admitting to being stumped so quickly.

The walls in Mr. Gibson's office were painted white and had nothing hanging on them. He certainly didn't want anyone to know anything about him. Or, Lucy considered, maybe he just didn't want to know about himself. Lucy opened one of his desk drawers. It was empty. "What does your dad do for work?" Lucy called out.

"He's some kind of consultant. I don't really know what that means, though," said Stella from the hallway outside Mr. Gibson's office door. "Have you found anything?"

Lucy opened another drawer and saw a yellow legal pad. That's when Mr. Gibson started pounding on the front door. Stella bit down on her fingernails. "Hurry up," she gasped.

The pounding got louder and the doorbell started going off like a cuckoo clock at midnight.

"Help Nicky keep your dad out of the apartment," said Lucy. "I'm almost done."

From the other room Lucy heard it loud and clear.

Mr. Gibson hollered, "NICKY!"

Oh my gosh, thought Lucy. *How did he get inside?*

10:55 a.m.

Before she ran to the front door, Stella yelled out to Lucy, "We're in such big trouble."

Lucy heard lots of yelling but tried to stay focused. There it was. Right in her hand. The evidence. Mr. Gibson had forged his mother's signature. But why? Lucy scurried down the long dimly lit hallway into the front foyer. She didn't know how Mr. Gibson had gotten inside, and at the moment she didn't care. She handed Nicky the legal pad. "Here's your evidence," she said.

Mr. Gibson stopped yelling to look at Lucy. Stella stopped crying to take a breath, and Nicky stared in disbelief at the legal pad. "But this is blank."

"Are you crazy?" asked Stella. "Why did we let you in here?"

Lucy glanced over at Nicky for reassurance, but he was shaking his head. "I'm kind of scared. My parents don't act like this," she said.

"Don't worry," said Nicky. "He won't hurt you."

Mr. Gibson rubbed his forehead and then took a step in Lucy's direction. She jumped back.

"There are impressions all over this piece of paper. 'Zelda Gibson's everywhere, like someone was practicing her signature." Lucy talked quickly.

"I don't see any," said Nicky.

"It's time for you to go home," huffed Mr. Gibson. "I think you've caused enough trouble."

Her first big case. She had practically solved it. She had to tell them what she'd found. "I didn't find the actual piece of paper that had the practice signatures on it, but it doesn't matter. We have the piece of paper that was under it, and that's good enough." She pulled a penlight from her back pocket and shined it onto the paper. "Look. Can you can see them, the impressions? See? It happens because of the pressure from the pen. The paper is like a writing fossil. There are clues all over it. The signatures at the bottom of the page look a lot more like Zelda Gibson's real signature than the ones at the top of the page, but they still don't match it. They do match the signature on the deed that you showed me."

Lucy removed a pencil from behind her right ear and colored in the corner of the page. Under the leaden gray the words "Zelda Gibson" suddenly materialized in yellow. They were barely visible, but they were there. "Zelda Gibson" after "Zelda Gibson." "Do you see what I'm talking about now?" she asked.

"That's amazing," said Nicky.

"Oh, my gosh," gasped Stella.

"There are probably about a hundred of them," said Lucy.

Mr. Gibson glared at Lucy.

"Dad," said Stella, "why did you do this?"

Mr. Gibson's throat sputtered and gurgled, like

he had lost his loud voice. He reflexively thought about sending Nicky to his room for a time-out. Instead he stared at Nicky's face for several uninterrupted minutes, almost like he had gone into a trance. Then he looked at Stella. She was wearing mascara and eyeliner. He wondered when she had started doing that. How strange that he didn't know.

Mr. Gibson rubbed his eyes in an attempt to rub out the last two years, or maybe the last ten, he wasn't sure.

"Maybe I'll go home now," said Lucy.

"Thanks for your help. I guess I'll see you in the elevator sometime," said Nicky.

"Yeah," said Lucy. "I hope so."

Nicky turned around and faced his father. "Dad? Tell us. Where's Grandma Zelda?"

Mr. Gibson spoke slowly and softly. "Okay, I will."

The three of them walked into the dining room. Mr. Gibson wiped the gathering beads of sweat off his forehead and opened the window. They sat at the dining room table together for the first time since Nicky's mother had left. After a long silence and several false starts, Mr. Gibson spoke.

"After your mother left, I couldn't work. I couldn't focus." He inhaled and wheezed, then continued. If there's one thing that grown-ups hate to do, it's tell their own children that they have done terrible things. Not just bad but awful. Mr. Gibson told Nicky and Stella the many bad things he'd done. He didn't so much make a list; it was more like a giant one-eyed ogre of a run-on confession. At the end of it he said, "One by one my clients left, and I felt like everyone had abandoned me. I was hurt and angry and started hurting everyone around me. Things were getting worse, not better, the longer your mother stayed away. The truth is, I wasn't very nice to your mom. I suppose I've never been nice to anyone. I haven't been terribly nice to you kids."

"Or Grandma Zelda," added Nicky.

"Or your grandmother. That's right," continued Mr. Gibson. "Maybe I've never known what it was like to be nice. I've never given it a try. Your grandmother had enough nice for everybody in the family. I suppose I felt that if I were going to get noticed, I'd have to find another way."

"What kind of excuse for being a total jerk is that?" asked Stella.

"Don't call Dad a jerk," said Nicky.

"It's okay. She's right. We're out of money. Broke. I lost all our money. Your grandmother, she's lived a long life. She always finds a way to get by. I decided to sell her apartment because I needed money. I'm not proud. Yes, I forged her signature. I forced her to leave."

"So where is she?" asked Nicky.

Mr. Gibson gulped. "I left her in the park. I'm sorry."

"You did what?" exclaimed Nicky. "You left her alone in the park? I feel sick. I'm getting out of here. You deserve a time-out!"

"You deserve a whole lot worse than that!" yelled Stella.

Mr. Gibson looked down at his hands. Nicky stood up to leave. Stella screeched. She was the first one to notice that a pigeon had flown into the dining room.

11:15 a.m.

Pigeon headed directly toward Nicky.

"What are you doing inside?" he asked.

"Every rule has an exception," she said quietly,

and dropped a piece of paper onto the table in front of him. She circled the room and flew out the same window she had entered—well, first she deposited a little something on top of Mr. Gibson's head.

Nicky picked up the piece of paper.

My Dearest Nicky and Stella,

A special winged friend found me. I don't know what my future looks like; one rarely does when they're my age. Perhaps my only son thinks I'd prefer to live in the park rather than in my own apartment. I'm afraid he's badly mistaken, but here I am, and I've made some lovely new friends.

I've been waiting for the right moment, and it occurs to me that the moment is now. It's my honor to bequeath to you, while I am still living, my beloved viola d'amore. I believe that every one of its fourteen strings is infused with a bit of magic. I've kept this a secret from you until now. You probably didn't think your grandma Zelda was capable of keeping secrets,

*but this one I held close to my heart. An artisan
prince handcrafted the viola d'amore in the
year 1780. The instrument is worth a fair sum
of money, should you choose to sell it. Use the
millions it will fetch at auction to pursue your
passions and loves, and never forget to live life.*

Your devoted grandma,

Zelda

Nicky read the note first, then handed it to Stella. She read it three times. Each reading was punctuated with the question, "Did that pigeon just fly in with this note?" Mr. Gibson left the room to clean himself up. (He could have used a good shower but settled for hot water and a soapy washcloth.)

When Mr. Gibson returned, Stella handed him the note.

"Dad, I want to sell the viola d'amore to pay your bills. Grandma Zelda needs to come home," said Nicky.

Stella looked over at Nicky and nodded in agreement.

Mr. Gibson sort of smiled. His voice still boomed, but he didn't sound quite as scary. "I'll agree to let you sell your grandmother's viola d'amore to help get us through this period, but I'm paying you both back. At the very least, I owe that to the two of you."

"Grandma Zelda's coming home," cheered Nicky. "I don't care about the rest."

Mr. Gibson stood up. His belly remained too large for his legs, and they wobbled for a second before he gained his balance. "Stella, why don't you go upstairs and get your grandmother's apartment ready for her? Nicky, let's go to the park and find her."

"Dad," said Nicky, "you're the best."

"Not really," said Mr. Gibson.

Nicky corrected himself, even though he knew it meant risking getting a new time-out. "You're right. You're a long way from the best, but right now you're not the worst."

"Thanks, son," said Mr. Gibson.

Noon
Riverside Park

Mr. Gibson and Nicky got out of the taxi on 116th Street and crossed into the park. Nicky careened down a steep hill while his father took the stairs. The park showed signs of spring, with blasts of colorful flowers that had sprouted prematurely. Mr. Gibson directed Nicky to the spot where he had left Grandma Zelda. "I hope she's still here," he said.

Bicyclists, Rollerbladers, skateboarders, dog walkers, and running children made navigating the crowded park something of a challenge. Nicky ran deeper into the park. He barely avoided a girl, who looked to be his age, walking a Great Dane and a tiny Chihuahua, and he stumbled over a fallen branch.

Then he spotted them, an old lady on a park bench sitting with a pigeon—the two of them surrounded by hundreds of sparrows.

Nicky took off like a torpedo toward his grandmother and threw his arms around her. He dropped his head onto her shoulder. He hugged her long and hugged her tight. The sparrows took flight, but Pigeon remained. "Thank you," whispered Nicky to Pigeon. Pigeon bobbed her head and cooed.

After he let her go from his hug, Grandma Zelda clutched on to her purse with one hand and held on to Nicky with the other. "Do I have an April Fools' story for you," she said.

"You knew the day you went missing was April Fools' Day?" asked Nicky.

"Of course I did, dear," replied Grandma Zelda.

By this time Mr. Gibson had caught up with them and stood off to the side watching.

"I'm sure this was all just a big joke." Grandma Zelda's left eye winked, as it so often did, and Mr. Gibson mouthed the words "Thank you."

Nicky held on tightly to his grandmother's hand. He helped her up and showed her the way home.

2:20 p.m.
West 68th Street, Apartment 6D

Dear Everyone,

I solved my first big case! I can't wait to tell you all about it in person. My parents told me we're coming to Savannah for two weeks this summer! I am so excited. We won't be moving back, but that's okay too. It's

really not that bad here. I hope
someday you will all come to
visit me.

Love,

Your friend and former
classmate, Lucy

APOLOGIES

To all sparrows,

My heartfelt apology if you feel maligned by this story.
I think that you, sparrows, are adorable. So why did I
write a character who feels differently? I suppose my
answer can be gleaned from a modified version of an
oft-quoted line from *The Godfather*, a movie that most
readers of this book are too young to watch.

"It's not personal, Sparrow. It's strictly business."

Apologies,

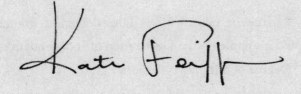

SIGNATURE TEST

1. Which of the two Thomas Jefferson signatures below was done by a forger?

Degree of difficulty: Easy

A.

B.

2. True or false: This is how Benjamin Franklin signed his name on the Declaration of Independence.

Degree of difficulty: Medium

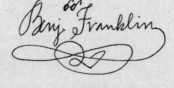

3. John Hancock has one of the most recognizable signatures in the world. Can you recognize which John

Hancock is from the Declaration of Independence and which two were done by a modern-day forger?

Degree of difficulty: Hard

A.

B.

C.

4. Two of these signatures have been forged. One is real. Can you guess which one belongs to the former First Lady Eleanor Roosevelt and which two were done by the forger?

Degree of difficulty: Very hard

A.

B.

C.

ANSWERS:

1. Thomas Jefferson

If you answered:

A: You answered correctly. Nice job.

B: Your answer is incorrect. Note the *J* in "Jefferson" looks more like a *G* than a *J*.

2. Benjamin Franklin

If you answered false, you are correct. You are good

at detecting forgeries. Benjamin Franklin did indeed invent bifocal glasses, but he did not draw a set of spectacles along with his signature on the Declaration of Independence.

3. John Hancock

If you answered:

A: This answer is correct. You are very good at detecting forgeries. John Hancock used a quill to sign his name on the Declaration of Independence.

B: You guessed wrong. Not only did the forger use a modern-day pen, she spelled Hancock incorrectly.

C: You guessed wrong. John Hancock is spelled correctly, but the forger did not use a quill pen and, as a result, almost all of the lines are the same width and thickness.

4. Eleanor Roosevelt

If you answered:

A: You guessed wrong. Look at the spelling of Roosevelt. Mrs. Roosevelt would never spell her name wrong. This forger forgot an *o*.

B: You got the right answer. You are an excellent detector of forgeries!

C: You guessed wrong. Notice the dot on the end of Roosevelt. The forger likely left her pen on the paper while looking back at her work. Also the *E* in "Eleanor" has a loop in it. Mrs. Roosevelt generally started her *E* with a line, not a loop.

For more signature tests go to signedbyzelda.com.

HOW TO MAKE A ZELDABERRY PIE

Sixty-two years ago, long before Grandma Zelda became a grandma, she started baking pies. At first she worked from a recipe that she found in a magazine, but over the years the recipe got stained and smeared and torn and eventually disappeared. (Somehow it got baked into a pie.) Since then, she's been baking from memory. Grandma Zelda's memory is a bit faulty these days, but her pies are always delicious. Here, to the best of her recollection, is how she does it.

TOOLS

Says Grandma Zelda:

"Yes, you'll need a few things, but don't waste daylight fretting if you don't have them all. If you can find your way around town without a map, you can cook without a rolling-pin sleeve."

1 flat board
1 pastry cloth
1 rolling pin
1 rolling-pin sleeve
1 pie dish
1 fork

2 large bowls

4 sandwich bags

1 pastry brush

measuring cups

measuring spoons

mixer

INGREDIENTS

Says Grandma Zelda:

"Make sure that no berry bush feels ignored or over-picked. Did I ever tell you about the time I kayaked across a lake to a small deserted island to pick low-bush blueberries and forgot to tie up my kayak? I was stuck on that island for eight days, but the blueberries were worth it. These days, all of my berries get delivered to my apartment."

4 cups all-purpose flour

1 teaspoon salt

½ cup cold water

2 eggs

1 tablespoon white vinegar

1½ cups shortening, like Crisco

½ stick very cold butter

⅓ cup sugar

3 shakes of cinnamon

5 cups of your choice of mixed berries. They can include blueberries, raspberries, strawberries, boysenberries, blackberries, and/or huckleberries.

MAKING PIE CRUST

Says Grandma Zelda:

"If this is biting off more than you can chew, you can go buy the pre-mades and then follow steps 8–16 of this recipe. But if you want to try making your own crust, I declare this is the recipe to follow. It takes practice, though. I think everything worthwhile does."

RECIPE

1. Wash hands, then dry them by shaking the water off.

2. In a large bowl mix the following ingredients together until crumbly, *not* smooth and silky: 3 ⅔ cup flour, the salt, the cold water, the egg, the white vinegar, the shortening, and the butter.

3. Remove from the bowl and shape into a large ball.

4. Cut the ball into four sections and put each section into a small plastic bag.

5. Wash hands again.

6. Use the clean palm of one hand to push down on

each of the bags until they are nice and flat and round.

7. Put the bags in the refrigerator for at least half an hour.

8. Prepare for the hard part by clearing some counter space, covering a flat board with a pastry cloth, flouring it, then covering a rolling pin with a sleeve and flouring that. When you are ready, take one of the bags of dough out of the fridge and roll it out until it fits it into your pie dish.

9. Preheat oven to 425 degrees.

10. Mix the sugar, 2 tablespoons of flour, and a shake of cinnamon into the berries, then pour the berries into the pie crust.

11. Roll another dough ball out flat and cover the berries with it, making sure the sides overhang enough for crimping.

12. Press the tines of the fork into the outer edges of the two pie crusts until there is no seepage. Then use the same fork to poke holes (about four on each side, eight to ten in total) in the top of the crust.

13. Separate the egg and put a few drops of water into the egg yolk. Beat the egg yolk and water with the fork.

14. Use your pastry brush to paint the top of the crust with the egg yolk–water mixture.

15. Bake at 425 degrees for 15–20 minutes.

16. Turn down the heat to 350 degrees and bake for 20 more minutes until the pie looks golden brown and shiny.

17. Take pie out of the oven and place on cooling rack. Let stand for 20 to 40 minutes, or until cool to the touch.

Enjoy!

AUTHOR'S NOTE

There was so much I wanted to talk about while writing this book, but very few people read a book before it's finished and it was difficult to find people to talk to. I tried talking to my family, but my family often likes to talk about things other than the book I'm working on. I went to New York to talk to my editor. She always seemed eager to discuss the book, but sometimes other authors were anxiously waiting to talk to her about their books, which meant I couldn't stay in her office talking for the two or three days I would have liked to. I finally resorted to talking to my dog, Henry, who occasionally sighed loudly, as if to indicate that I'd be a lot more interesting if I talked while scratching his belly.

When *Signed by Zelda* gets published, I imagine I will still be eager to talk about it, and if there are readers who would like to talk about it too, here are some of the topics I propose we discuss.

The Idea for the Book

My neighbor Alan Robillard is a retired FBI agent. I highly recommend living next door to a former FBI agent, especially one as nice as Alan, when looking for an idea for a book. Alan was once the chief of the Questioned Documents Unit at the FBI and he currently works as a forensic questioned document expert. He is often asked to determine whether a signature on an official document is authentic or forged.

One of the cases Alan worked on involved the wealthy philanthropist Brooke Astor. Alan was asked to give his opinion about a signature on a revision to her will. Had it been forged? I was intrigued by this case. Mrs. Astor's son, Anthony Marshall, had been accused of trying to steal millions of dollars from her estate, there was a mystery surrounding a signature, and, as if that weren't enough to get my attention, her grandson Philip had turned on his own father to protect his grandmother.

I found myself thinking about Philip, Mrs. Astor's grandson. Philip had exposed his father as a heartless heel and opened him up to the charges that were filed against him. I wondered how difficult it was for him to turn against his father. I thought about this so much that I started concocting different scenarios that might lead a son to turn on his father. If your father robbed a bank, would you turn him in? (Yes? No? Not sure?) If your father started a forest fire, would you turn him in?

(Yes? No? Not sure?) If your father hit a dog, tripped a blind man, or jumped a turnstile, would you turn him in? I was spending so much time thinking about this that I decided to write a book about a boy who believes that his father may have done something terrible. Of course, the boy doesn't know for sure until he discovers if a signature on a legal document is real or forged.

Graphology

Graphology is the study of handwriting. A graphologist looks for clues to someone's personality by analyzing their handwriting. Graphology is different from the forensic study of handwriting. Lucy is interested in both graphology and forensics. Someday she will be a full-service handwriting expert. While I browsed some of the many websites about graphology, I did most of my research using these three books: *Sex, Lies, and Handwriting: A Top Expert Reveals the Secrets Hidden in Your Handwriting* by Michelle Dresbold with James Kwalwasser; *The Definitive Book of Handwriting Analysis* by Marc Seifer, PhD; and *Handwriting Analysis: Putting It to Work for You* by Andrea McNichol with Jeffrey A. Nelson. Jan Leach wrote an article titled "Under Lines," which I found online, in which she points out that when Eleanor Roosevelt signed her name, the *R* in her "Roosevelt" was larger than the *E* in "Eleanor," symbolizing Mrs. Roosevelt's pride in the former first family's accomplishments. I also contacted Mark Seifer, whose book I referred to often, and he generously shared his insights into the handwriting of several Revolutionary War figures.

Forensic Questioned Document Examiner

Forensic handwriting examiners use scientific methodology to arrive at conclusions about the authenticity of handwriting that is under dispute. Through their examination, they can reveal details about the type of writing implement used and the source of the paper a document was written on. One of the tools forensic handwriting examiners use is an electrostatic detection device. These devices seem to magically illuminate notations on what looks like a blank piece of paper by revealing any impressions on the paper. Since these devices can cost thousands of dollars, Lucy relied on less expensive and more universally accessible methods to reveal indented writing. She used pencil shading and the holding of a flashlight onto it at an oblique angle. Give it a try. Get a notebook and sign your name a few times, then take the page underneath and shine the light from a flashlight at a 45-degree angle onto it. Now take a pencil and shade the page using the side, not the point, of the lead. For research on the forensics of handwriting, I consulted Alan Robillard, my neighbor, who always made time to explain things to me.

The Location

Signed by Zelda takes place in a city much like New York City. It is so much like New York that it is called New York, but as everyone who lives in New York or grew up in New York, as I did, knows, the city in the book is not exactly New York. The building that Nicky, Grandma Zelda, and Lucy live in on West 68th isn't a real building. Nicky's and Lucy's schools aren't real schools. While there are many similarities to the real New York City, this New York isn't an exact replica of the real deal.

Pigeon

Pigeons are an intriguing and often maligned bird with a valiant history. In his fascinating book titled *Pigeons*, Andrew D. Blechman writes that it was pigeons that transported the results of the first Olympic games and the news of Napoléon Bonaparte's defeat at Waterloo.

Pigeons can fly vast distances at high speeds. Pigeon in *Signed by Zelda* is not based on one real pigeon; she is a compilation of pigeons I have watched in my life.

The Viola d'Amore

My grandmother Claire Sheftel Kroyt played the viola d'amore. The instrument is about the size of a viola but has two sets of strings, one tucked away below the other. I am lucky enough to have a viola d'amore that my grandmother played.

I could certainly go on and on, but I'll stop here. If you'd like to keep going, however, please stop by signedbyzelda.com.

DEED OF ACKNOWLEDGMENTS

I, Kate Feiffer ("Author"), hereby thank the following people for their help and support during the writing of this book:

Maddy Alley ("Favorite Daughter"), for her spot-on editorial advice over the course of several drafts of this book.

Chris Alley ("Favorite Husband"), for always being sweet and available to pick up the pieces and pick up Favorite Daughter.

Paula Wiseman ("Wonderful Editor"), for gently and brilliantly directing this book through what Author estimates is close to two million and six revisions. Wonderful Editor's insights consistently cultivated the gem in the rough.

Alan Robillard ("Forensic Questioned Document Examiner"), for his explanations and inspiration. Also for his wife, Judy; they are wonderful neighbors.

Meryl Gordon ("Author Mrs. Astor Regrets"), for allowing Author to sit in on fascinating interview with Forensics Questioned Document Examiner. In many ways, out of that day came this story.

Anne Ausubel ("Baker"), for the pie recipe. What an unexpected gift it is to have met Baker.

Mike Remer ("Attorney"), for watching Author's back and for your wise counsel and support. You are missed.

Nicole Galland, Melissa Hackney, Laura Roosevelt, and Catherine Walthers ("Well-fed Writer's Group"), for providing magnificent insights that consistently help make the writing stronger.

Mrs. Brown's fourth-grade class ("sensational signatories") for their signatures.

Sam Fleming, Sarah Hill, Cindy Kane, and Lauren Martin ("Zelda Cheering Squad"), for being my rocks.

Ciara and James Seccombe ("Young Readers"), for agreeing to read early versions of *Zelda*.

Pat and Kerry Alley ("Favorite In-laws"), for forever feeding Author, Favorite Daughter, and Favorite Husband delicious food and delightful conversation.

Megan Adams ("Calligrapher Extraordinaire"), for her handwriting and friendship.

Jules Feiffer ("Favorite Father"), to whom I will someday give a copy of this book, and Judy Feiffer ("Favorite Mother"), for always being there to talk.

With love, admiration, and respect for each of you,

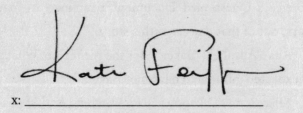

x: _____